the
man
who
looked
like
the
prince
of
wales

Books by
Frederick Manfred

NOVELS

The Golden Bowl 1944
This Is The Year 1947
The Chokecherry Tree 1948
Morning Red 1956
The Man Who Looked Like The
Prince of Wales 1965

RUMES

Boy Almighty 1945
Wanderlust * 1962

STORIES

Arrow of Love 1961

TALES

Lord Grizzly 1954
Riders of Judgment 1957
Conquering Horse 1959
Scarlet Plume 1964

❋

A new revised edition
of a trilogy that was
originally published
in three separate volumes:
The Primitive, 1949,
The Brother, 1950,
The Giant, 1951.
Mr. Manfred wrote under the
pen name of Feike Feikema
from 1944 through 1951.

FREDERICK MANFRED

Trident Press

NEW YORK 1965

the
man
who
looked
like
the
prince
of
wales

to
Vardis
Fisher

*the
man
who
looked
like
the
prince
of
wales*

1

Free was almost asleep, when something Pa said
made him wide awake again.

Pa said, "The trouble with Garrett is, he can't
leave it alone."

"Shhh," Ma said, "you don't have to talk so loud,
Alfred."

"Well, it's still true. Garrett couldn't leave it
alone with that June Memling slip of a thing and
now here with this Laura Pipp chunk."

"I think the stair door is open a little," Ma said.
"Free is at that age now where he has ears a mile
long."

"The stair door's closed," Pa said shortly. "I closed it myself. When I sent him to bed." Pa stamped around in the kitchen. "Yep, Garrett can't leave it alone. That's his trouble. It's in him like rot in an orchard. Spring comes along, and there's lots of blossoms, and you think you're gonna get a good apple this year, but come August there it is again. The brown-spot rot."

"Must you talk so loud, Alfred? I think you better close that door to the living room. Free can still hear us through the register around the stovepipe, I think."

"What difference does it make if he does hear it anyway? He knows all about what them four-legged pigs do out in the barnyard already, so what he learns about the two-legged pigs in the houseyard won't hurt him any."

"There is a difference," Ma said, sadly. "Close the door."

Pa's heels drummed on the linoleum floor a half-dozen steps and then the door to the dining room closed with a flat slam.

Free rolled over on his back and pushed his pillow down and away from his ear to hear better. Pa and Ma were still talking but now he couldn't make out a word. First there was a deep rumbling from Pa and then there was a soft mumbling from Ma. And whenever Everett, Free's younger brother and bed

4

partner, heaved a long deep sigh, he couldn't even hear that.

Free was at last very wide awake in the darkness. What in God's name had Garrett done? "The trouble with Garrett is, he can't leave it alone." Garrett was their hired man; though really he was more a member of the family than he was a hand. Garrett was an Engleking, like Ma, and her full cousin. Before Ma got married her name had been Ada Engleking. Or really Adelheid Engleking.

Free thought Garrett was a great man. Free had been mad at Garrett a couple of times, yes sure, because Garrett had bawled him out for being a lazy ass, for not getting the cobs in the fuelbox for Ma, and the eggs, and for not getting the evening chores started so Pa and Garrett could work longer in the field, and the milking, sure. But Garrett had also taken a lot of time showing him how to hold a baseball bat and swing flat level at the ball. Garrett had also given him a pair of wonderful leather mittens to wear to school to drive Tip with because he'd curried Garrett's driving horse Lady real good. When Garrett did things with him, together, it was always a game; would they make it or wouldn't they make it. Like that time when all of a sudden that yellow blizzard came up and Garrett came on horseback to school to get them, and while they didn't make it home to Pa they did make it home to Garrett's pa,

Big John Engleking by the Little Rock River. Or like that time when they hurried to have the chores done before Pa and Ma came home from Gramma's and they made it, just, with the milk pails still dripping water a little from the racks by the gate.

Garrett always slept in the other bed across the room, with little brother Flip. Free held his breath and listened a minute. Yep, Flip was sleeping all right. But Garrett was gone. Garrett hadn't come home yet. Probably out busy with whatever it was Pa was talking about. Wonder what it was Garrett couldn't leave alone? Could he be playing with himself like them Pipp boys did? No, because he would do that by himself and so nobody would know. Anyway, Garrett was big like Pa, and Pa didn't do things like that. Pa was Pa.

Free lay listening, straining his ears. Yep, Pa was still jawing away about it downstairs in the kitchen and Ma still wasn't saying much.

Free just had to know what it was that Garrett had done, and he got an idea. If he was to somehow crawl into that low attic over the kitchen, where Pa'd stored some of the family trunks and pictures, right above where Pa and Ma were now, where the pipe from the kitchen stove came up through the rafters, he'd be sure to be able to hear them. It would take some doing though. And he'd have to be quieter than a mouse with skinned paws. Pa had ears like a blind stallion. Pa could sometimes hear a bubble break in your belly clear across church.

Free slipped out from under the covers and let his feet down easy onto the board floor. He slept in his underwear and like always it was already too small for him. Pa said he grew so fast he sometimes outgrew his clothes and shoes before they was bought. The right leg of the underwear had slipped up to his knee and he pulled it down over his calf. His arms stuck out, and in the chilly June night air he had sudden goose pimples.

Free tiptoed silently into the hall. He took the first step down the stairs and felt cautiously to his right. Good. The big two-by-twelve bridge plank rested as usual on its edge against the wall. He couldn't see it but he knew where the other end of it went—that it just reached across to the little door into the attic over the kitchen. He caught hold of the bridge plank and carefully, cautiously, tipped it toward him, letting it down flat very gently. So far so good. He got on it, hands and knees, and began crawling toward the attic door. The plank was slightly warped, and as he approached the low door the plank moved under him, tilting somewhat, until it lay flat ahead. He crawled along until his brush of hair touched the low door. He sat back, carefully unhooked the latch, pulled the door open. No squeaks. And Pa's talking came to him as clear as a bell ringing inside a church. The air breathing out of the attic was strong with the smell of smoked wood. There was also something that smelled stuffily sweet. As Free's foot left the warped plank, the plank tipped back to its original level. There was a very low boom of a sound.

Free caught his breath.

Pa kept right on talking below.

Good. It meant Pa hadn't heard.

Free remembered that the floor in the kitchen attic was just loose boards. The boards were probably all warped too, like the plank was, and would move under him if he wasn't careful. Well, this was no place for horseplay. Yet sitting in the low doorway all cramped up was no good either. The best place to listen was near where the pipe from the kitchen came through. There he'd also be sure to hear what Ma had to say.

One knee and one hand at a time he crept across the attic. His left shoulder brushed against a big wooden trunk. It was where Ma kept a bunch of old letters. Next his right shoulder bumped into a packed sack of something. He sniffed the sack. Then he gave it a pinch. There was a soft sound, like fine sand crunching on itself. Sugar. So this was where Pa kept the extra sugar. Ha. Everett used to sneak licks of sugar when Pa kept the sack in the north room. Free moved on. He picked up several slivers in the palms of his hands from the raw floor boards. Soon heat from the stovepipe breathed over him. That felt fine. It was no good sitting in the chilly night air with just his underwear on. He turned to sit. The board under his right hand gave off a quick high-pitched squeak.

Free sat very still, eyes wide. He saw little prickly stars in the dark.

"Shhh," Ma said. Her voice came up very clear past the stovepipe.

"What," Pa said.

"I heard something."

"Where?"

"In the attic."

"Probably them fetch-sticking mice getting at the sugar again," Pa said. "And I set traps all over the place."

Traps? Free thought: "Boy! was I lucky I didn't hit any of them in the dark."

Ma sighed, exasperated.

Free smiled to himself. Ma was probably thinking about them mouse turds in the sugar again.

Pa said, "Though personal, I ain't satisfied but what it wasn't them blame kids again. They sure like to lick sugar off the table when you ain't lookin'."

Silence.

"Well, I don't hear it again," Pa said.

"Maybe I was just hearing things," Ma said.

There was a sound of pouring below. That was

Pa helping himself to a good-night cup of coffee. Free could see him just as plain. Pa always stood tall over the stove, long leg up on the reservoir, black hair turning white shining in the lamplight, eyes burning a little like a car's headlights.

Ma sighed.

"Well, as I was saying," Pa said, "Garrett wanted us to be the first to know. He said since he was working for us an' all, he owed it to us not to have it come from someone else first."

"At least his heart is in the right place."

Pa snorted. "Where else did you expect it to be? In his ass?"

"Alfred. Such terrible rough language."

"It's a man's language."

"Alfred."

Pa took a loud sip. "Yep. The trouble with Garrett is, he can't leave it alone."

Free let down in the dark and sat easy. Good. They were still talking about what Garrett had done. Now maybe he would find out what it was.

"I asked him how it happened this time," Pa said, "but he wouldn't say."

"I don't understand it," Ma said. "I just simply don't understand it. You'd think after what happened with that June Memling girl he'd know better, that he'd at least wait until he was married again."

"Some men can't wait."

10

"A Christian man should be able to."

"Ha! Even some of them saints couldn't wait. The way I heard it."

"A covenant child behaves himself."

Pa said slyly, "Well, it's in the Engleking blood. They've all got that hot hair. Every last one of 'em."

Ma said quietly, "Your present wife too?"

"Well, no, that I can't say. I guess."

Free could just see Ma staring Pa down. Ma wasn't fierce like Pa. She was kind. But that made it all the worse. She had gold hair and quiet blue eyes, and she could make her tongue wait and wait, and then would come that sad suffering tough look and you felt awful. You couldn't do enough for her then, even though you hated what you did for her with all you had in you. Ma hated all talk about breeding and such stuff. While Pa was always talking about it. They often argued about it.

This time Ma also spoke her mind. "I notice you Alfredsons ain't so slow either. Hehh. You wasn't named Alfred Alfredson VI for nothing. All them generations with always the firstborn a boy."

"Pah. That ain't got nothing to do with it."

"Those poor mothers all those generations. I looked up your family tree once. Upstairs in that old family Bible. The boy babies outnumbered the girl babies ten to one. And now look at us here. Three already and no girls. God knows what this next one will be."

Pa sobered. "I probably shouldn't've brought it up the way you're feeling. The bad news."

"What's the difference? I would have learned of it anyway."

Pa took a modest sip of coffee.

"And Free's wild ways . . . hehh! I suppose as Alfred VII he's gonna be a breeder of male sons too."

"Now, Ada."

"You men make me sick."

"All them Engleking men make you sick too?" Pa rose a little. "Ha! They ain't called the trembling Englekings for nothing. With their white-gold hair flashing in the sun."

There was a small noise like Ma might be opening her patching box. She was always fixing the family's clothes after the supper dishes were done.

Free had on occasion watched himself to see if he trembled when he got mad or excited. Some of the Englekings trembled something fierce. Garrett wasn't half as bad as his younger brother Al. Both were great ball players, but sometimes in a close game Al trembled so hard he couldn't bat, while Garrett still could and hit good too. In a tight place the Englekings got too choked up, turned black almost. Such times, with their flashing gold hair, they were quite a sight.

12

Pa said, "I've often wondered about something. That gold hair and that trembling goes all through your relations. Like maybe there was a stud grampa somewhere back there who had it so deep in his blood it was stronger than what he bred into. I had a Poland China boar once that did that. He had a white eye and I'll be darned if that white eye didn't show up the next spring in all the litters as a pink eye. Not only did I have to get rid of him, I had to get rid of his gilts too, and start over. If I wanted to have the pedigree papers for 'em, they said."

"Please, no cursing now."

"Wonder if the Prince of Wales trembles like that. And has that exact same gold hair. If he does, then maybe he is related to you Englekings after all. Far back."

Ma said nothing.

"That Prince of Wales fellow. You know. The one who's Garrett's age."

Ma said nothing.

"You Englekings coming from East Friesland in Germany like that and that English king's family coming from where they did, them places ain't too far apart."

Ma worked at her patching.

"Well, a lot a good it's done Garrett to look like him. It's got him into nothing but trouble, that's a fact."

13

Ma said nothing.

"Yeh, the trouble with Garrett is, he can't leave it alone."

Ma asked, "How did Garrett act when he told you about it?"

"Well, for once, he wasn't trembling. But he sure was red."

"What did he say again?"

"Well, he commenced to fidgeting around while we was milking, and then finally he came out with it. He says, 'Alf, I got some bad news again I think.' I says, 'How so?' He says, 'Well, Alf, Laura Pipp is going to have a baby.' I says, 'Nah!' He says, 'Yes, and I'm just about going crazy inside. You know what happened to the other one.' You remember June Memling died right after she had that blue baby born dead. I says, 'I remember all right. How does Laura take it?' He says, 'She's all right. But she's afraid to tell her pa. Because he told her once he wouldn't let her marry me.' I says, 'Do you love her?' He says, 'I think so. But, boy, it's going to be hard to stand up in that church again and admit fornication a second time. Boy, sometimes I feel like running away.' I says, 'Now, that ain't gonna do you any good. Be a man and face up to it.' He says, 'Yes, easier said than done.'"

Free listened a mile a minute. So that's what Garrett'd done. He'd knocked up another girl. Before

14

they got married. It made Free nervous to think about it. It was an awful thing to do to a girl when she didn't want it.

Lately Free'd had trouble with the word "it." Every time Pa said, "Did you do it," meaning, did you get the cows, Free would shiver, thinking Pa meant, "Did you play with yourself again?" Or when Garrett said, "Stick it in," meaning, put the bolt through the hole there you dumb fool, Free would shiver, thinking Garrett meant, "Stick it into that neighbor girl Gertie."

"Poor Garrett," Ma said. "He must feel just awful both asleep and awake."

"Hey," Pa said, "it sounds now like you're ready to excuse what he done. And here I thought you'd be madder'n——"

"Poor Garrett. Well, he must be worth fighting over if the Devil works that hard to get him."

"Pots and damnation!"

"We must pray for Garrett," Ma said. "It's going to be hard enough for him to stand up before the congregation again. Very hard. But do it he must, and we must pray for him and hope that the good Lord will sustain him in his hour of trial."

Pa set his coffee cup down with a light bang. "Ada, you like him."

"I feel sorry for him. He has a good heart, really. Look how good he is with our kids. He's really a good, kind man. If it wouldn't be for this craze of his for girls, he'd be a saint. A soft man, and good."

Pa snorted. "Soft is right. Best wellman and plumber we had around here, and yet he didn't know enough to collect his bills. Went busted. Let every Tom, Dick and Harry charge at his store, including them no-good bum Coopers, who never did pay up their debts the last town they lived in. I'll bet Garrett's got over ten thousand outstanding he could still collect." Pa whacked his coffee cup down again. "When you run a hardware store, by God, you got to run it cash on the barrelhead, and nothing but! And when you go out and fix somebody's well, same thing. Cash. 'Cause credit's the ruination of the world."

"It's because Garrett's got a good heart. And can't say no."

"Pah! It's more because he's got a soft head, I say." Pa poured himself some more coffee. "Though I have to admit he's a hard worker. His loss goin' busted in that hardware store was our gain. He's the best hired hand I ever had."

"Garrett and Laura mustn't wait until it's too late again. They both better confess and get it over with and get married. As soon as possible. Poor June Memling."

"Man, man, won't them hypocrites over in the Big Christian Church point the finger at us Little Christian Churchers now. 'See,' they'll say, 'you Little

Christian Churchers think you're so good, the one true Church and all, think you're so much closer to Christ—ha! look at what your young people do at night between the corn rows, hey?'" Pa dropped his foot to the floor. "And they're right. And all because one of our Engleking's got a hot hair."

"Alf."

"It's the truth." Pa finished off his second cup of coffee with a loud swallow.

"Poor Garrett."

Pa turned sly again. Free could see Pa's face become a mask of mock gravity. "Though there are times I sure wished some of that hot trembling blood could've showed up in the Engleking women. Only the Engleking men seem to have it."

Free thought: "That's a dirty trick for Pa to say that. Pa knows Ma's sister, Aunt Joan, got knocked up and had to get married. Pa knows about Allie, Ma's cousin, Garrett's older sister, before Allie got married to Frank Westing, how Allie was caught doing it with Willie Alfredson up in the haymow, and on Sunday yet, in the afternoon when everybody else was to church."

Free thought: "I sure like to play ball with Garrett. He's a lot of fun. And real good too. But I'm going to feel funny when he asks me after supper if I wanna knock up some flies with him."

"Poor Garrett," Ma sighed. "Well, when you see

17

him in the morning, if he comes home tonight, tell him I'm praying for him."

"Ha. That ain't what the church consistory is gonna say. At least not at first. That's a fact. They may even kick him out of the church for the time bein'."

After a while Pa announced he was tired. He went outside, peedoodled on the grass by the gate, and stomped off to bed.

It took Ma a little longer. She had a big stomach and she groaned over it.

While Ma was out in the privy, Free crawled back to bed. He was careful to set the two-by-twelve bridge plank up on edge like he'd found it. It felt good to be back in bed beside Everett again.

2

Garrett picked up the reins from where he had wrapped them around the butt of the whip. "What's the matter, Lady?"

Lady was a flashy chestnut pacer. She had seen something in the moonlight. Both her ears were shot ahead and her easy swinging lateral gait had suddenly mounted into a high-toed prance. Lady turned her head from side to side to look past her blinkers, first with one eye and then the other.

"Easy, girl. Easy, now."

Garrett stared ahead too.

Moonlight glanced blackly off the arching steel

trusses of the plank bridge across the Little Rock River. Wild plum bushes grew in the ditch to the left, and it was from them that a quartet of wolves had once jumped Garrett and Lady. Lady had sensed them then, had smelled them, and had started to shy off as if to whirl around in the middle of the road. But Garrett had held a stiff rein on her, made her head hold steady. Then, with a wild flutter of nostrils, a trumpet blast, Lady had dashed right through them, hooves striking high, buggy wheels clamoring on the loose planks of the bridge—and then Garrett and Lady were suddenly across and free. The four wolves followed them a ways, but they were hardly a match for Lady's speed. Lady could run.

Garrett remembered something else about that night. He had been on his way to see June Memling. He remembered he had made up his mind that night that they simply had to tell their parents about what they had done. Four weeks later, June was gone.

"Easy, now, girl. Don't let your mind run away with you. Those four wolves are long ago shot and killed."

Lady's head came up even higher. Celluloid rings glanced red and white from her slack checkrein. She listened so hard the tips of her ears almost came together in front. Then she let go a great fluttering trumpeting blast. There was something in those wild plum bushes after all.

Garrett popped squirrel-upright in his seat. The yellow silk duster over his knees slid to a heap at his feet. He held the lines steady. "Girl! Girl!"

Two figures popped out of the bushes. They were human, and with a quavering bloodcurdling shout they began waving blankets Indian fashion at Lady. They yowled like maniacal squaws.

Lady leveled, then plunged on, her sleek chestnut butt rolling with exploding bulges of power. It wasn't wolves after all. These two-leggeds couldn't slash at her hocks. They were only humans with short dull teeth. She held her nose high and rammed her broad chest straight into them. Her throwing forelegs ran them down. With a choked curse they fell away before her. Rattle-de-rumble on the bridge planks and she and Garrett were across.

Garrett allowed himself a smile, and relaxed on his buggy seat. He recognized one of the cursers. It was Bill Tamming. Bill and his brother Ted had said several times uptown in Bonnie that some night they would fix Garrett's clock for him.

The two Tamming boys lived west of the river on the hills to the right. Their Pa was a short subdued man; while their Ma was a huge haystack of a woman. Ma Tamming was one of those mothers who believed everything bad about her old man and everything good about her boys. The result was her boys often went hogwild. They were huge fellows with impassive wind-red faces, high noses, and wild blue eyes. When they decided they didn't like something they usually tore it all to pieces. If they felt like it, that is. The Englekings were not afraid of them, however, mostly because the Englekings outnumbered them, and also because their own Fat John was known as the strongest man in Leonhard County. Fat John had once taken his fist and knocked down a contrary mule with one punch. The Tammings were there when it happened. They said nothing. Only their wild blue eyes flashed in their wind-red impassive faces.

Garrett sighed, and fell sad again. If the Tamming boys only knew about him and Laura. If they only knew. Bill Tamming would go bull wild. Garrett reached down and drew the yellow duster up over his knees again.

At the turnoff into Bonnie, Garrett was startled to have Lady veer left, not right.

"Hey, what's this? You lost or something? Town's that way, girl." He unwrapped the lines once more from the stock of the buggy whip and gave her a correcting tug.

Lady's mouth resisted him. Stubbornly she set her arched neck against his tug and plunged the buggy, wheels sparkling silver in the moonlight, under the Cannonball railroad trestle.

"Not that way, you durn fool!" Garrett cried.

"What the dickens. I've got enough troubles without you adding to them." Garrett hauled upon both lines, hard. "Whoa, there. Whoa!" And pulling her muzzle tight against her chest, he stopped her.

He swore at her mildly. "I thought we was going to town to trade in that crate of eggs and get Alf and Ada some groceries? Remember? Then afters we was going to see the girl friend?" Garrett's gold hair flashed bronze. His face darkened to a warm red as he got a little mad.

Girl friend, yes. The direction Lady had taken certainly wasn't toward Laura Pipp's house. It was toward where June Memling lay buried in the Bonnie Cemetery up on the hills west of the Big Rock River.

"Darling June Memling, she died of the green gangrene."

Garrett had often gone there alone and sat at her headstone, while Lady cropped the rich grasses along the lanes between the graves.

Garrett sat very still in his buggy for a long moment.

Then, sighing, he said, "All right, Lady, all right. I'll let you have your head this time. We'll go pick a handful of eagle flowers and put them on June's grave. Pay our respects. Before we take up the new burden for the night."

Garrett knew where some eagle flowers, or col-

ness gave no credit. He had a way of making a go of it even if his store was the smaller one in town. He had six daughters; no sons. He was often asked how come he had no boys and as often shrugged his shoulders sheepishly as if to say he probably wasn't much of a man. His wife was a block of a woman and at all times indulged her six beautiful silver-haired daughters.

Beautiful and silver-haired they were, especially the oldest daughter June. June was a queen. She had a forehead shaped like an exquisite clamshell, a straight nose with perfectly belled nostrils, gently rounded cheekbones and chin, and teeth as even and as white as a new ivory comb. Her eyes were wild blue lupines. She was slender, and relaxed in manner and walk. When called, she turned her head very slowly, and slowly took one in, and never did get around to say hello. But when at last a smile widened her pink ribbonlike lips, it was response enough. When the Maker finished making June, he kept the mold handy for the Memling girls yet to come. The Memling girls could have been sextuplets.

Only the two older Memling girls were dateable, June and Marie. June was fifteen and Marie fourteen. The two girls threw Bonnie into a boil. The boys from both the Little Christian Church and the Big Christian Church went wild over them the first couple of months.

Presently it became apparent that while the Memling girls might have their parents' permission to date, they were pretty cool about using that permission. The first four Sundays they turned down fifty-six requests for dates. The boys in their snappy buggies went home pretty red-faced. The Tamming boys were turned down four times in a row.

Garrett, meanwhile, bided his time. He was an Engleking. He might tremble a little like the rest of the Engleking men when worked up, but crawl on his belly like a fawning puppy, no. Besides, one Saturday night at the Memling store he had suddenly found himself being measured by June's deep lupine eyes. She clerked for her father, and Garrett had gone in to buy a can of Prince Albert tobacco. While checking out a curved stem pipe, he felt something cool pass over him, like a door might've been left open somewhere, and when he turned to look, there she was, standing beside a bolt of red silk, quietly studying him. He smiled, and his blue eyes warmed, and he quickly ran his fingers through his gold pompadour. Her ribbon lips widened ever so slightly.

One Saturday night in late September just as she was leaving the store with her father, Garrett walked up dressed in a blue serge suit. "Good evening, Mr. Memling. Well, June, are you ready?"

She regarded him coolly. "It's not Sunday night."

"I don't like them Sunday night crowds. Are you ready?"

"It's late."

"My Lady thought maybe you'd like a ride home. You ready?"

June's slow blue eyes opened. "Lady?"

"My chestnut pacer. She's a dandy."

"All right." She turned to her father. "I'll ride with him, Pa."

Long John Memling didn't even bother to answer. He just turned his stooped frame around and swung his long legs for home.

Garrett took June's elbow and helped her into the buggy. As June settled herself, Lady turned her head around, high and arched, and gazed a single glowing eye at her.

Garrett smiled at Lady. "Like her already, doncha? Well, so do I." Then Garrett stepped into the buggy beside June. Deftly, still smiling, he spread the yellow duster over both their knees and tucked them in. He picked up the reins, gave them a little ripple, and off they went, Lady's lean rump breaking into a bobbing run, leather traces squeaking on the singletree.

Under a riding moon, buggy wheels spinning off four rolling webs of silver, he took her to where some plums still hung scarlet near the Big Rock south of town. Next he showed her where a rare shrub of wild bullberries grew. Then he showed her where a swatch of coneflowers thrived. Finally he showed her where the local lovers' lane was, northwest of Bonnie.

Lovers' lane ran from the Big Rock River to Mud Creek. Both sides of the road were fringed with chokecherry brush. Grass grew so deep it was hard to see the trail. It was almost two in the morning, yet no less than eight buggies were parked at various points along the lane.

Garrett pulled up Lady for a breather. They were on the east end of the lane, just off the rusting Faber bridge. "Shall we see who's spooning who?"

"Not tonight."

"No? Why not?"

"I might see some friends."

"All the more reason."

"Can't we let them have a few secrets?" June shook her long silver bob. "I know I want mine."

At that Garrett began to tremble. For all her coolness she was one of those then. "All right. If you say so."

Lady began to fidget between the shafts.

"See," June said, "even your chestnut knows better than to be nosy."

Garrett's teeth flashed white in the moonlight. "Lady's got itchy pants because there's a prize stud over at Miller's place. She smells him."

29

June sat still and silver.

"Well, then," Garrett said, "at least let me show you one of my secrets. My personal lovers' lane."

"No, thanks."

"Don't you want to see a really secret place?" Garrett's white sunburnt brows came together in a frown.

"No."

"It's like a little Garden of Eden there." Garrett got hold of his trembling and quieted it down.

"Out here on the prairie?"

Garrett smiled. "I'll show you. Hup there, Lady, this way."

"No." June flipped the yellow duster from her lap and got ready to step out of the buggy.

"Wait." Garrett blushed. Muscles under his suit jacket bulged. "There's no need for that." He tugged Lady's lines the other way, toward Bonnie. "The heck with it. I ain't never yet forced anybody to do what they didn't want to do."

"Good." June got under the silk duster with him again.

Lady's revolving hooves clip-clopped them to June's house in a couple of minutes.

Garrett was going to jump out and help June down, but she beat him to it. In a whip she was out from under the duster and on the ground. June surprised him. She had a motion like a bluebird coming in for a landing. Though stumped, Garrett still managed an Engleking smile. "I thought maybe you could give me a little kiss."

"Why?"

"Because of the way you looked at me in the store."

Silver silence.

"At least that."

As quickly as she'd got down, she got up into the buggy again. She leaned and kissed him. It was a dry kiss but it was also a firm kiss.

"Hey, how come you changed your mind?"

"You were right. I did look at you in the store that way. So there you are. Goodnight." Down she stepped again, as light as a bird, and the next thing Garrett knew the front door of her father's house had closed behind her and she was gone.

"I'll be cow-kicked."

Lady started up on her own and home they went.

Garrett let three weekends go by before he asked June again. This time he tried it on Sunday night, after Young People's Catechism. Quietly he hitched up his Lady, avoiding the other boys, and with a twiggle of his buggy whip, more for show than anything else since Lady never needed it, set off for downtown.

Girls in bunches of twos and threes, heads and

thighs close together, paraded up the walk toward town, emitting perfumes as they scuffed along. While up and down the boys rolled, whistling tunes, showing off, raising the dust. The girls watched the boys wheel by, and laughed subdued, and wondered who would ask who.

Garrett caught up with June just as she and her sister Marie turned off to go home. It was very dark out, almost too dark to see them. He drove Lady across the sidewalk, blocking the girls' path.

"Well," he said, "just in time, I see." Garrett'd be damned first before he'd ask the usual question: "May I take you home?"

"Well, well, it's Lady, I see." June spoke quietly. "Hello, Lady. Anybody been mean to you lately?"

Marie Memling was in a flutter. It was easy to see she thought more of Garrett than June did.

But Garrett had no eyes for Marie. He said, "We can drop Marie off after we take a little spin through town."

Marie's face fell.

June said, "I'm afraid Marie goes with the whole night."

Damn that Marie.

Garrett quickly masked his feelings. He smiled. One never caught an Engleking short. He wound up the reins and hopped out to help the girls aboard.

32

June took a seat beside Garrett and Marie sat on the outside.

They were about to ride off, when Garrett said, holding Lady up, "I have one rule. If it's women, once they're in this buggy, they got to kiss the driver."

"Always?" June challenged.

Marie shivered.

"Always," Garrett said. "When shall it be, now or later?"

"Now," June said. Quickly she kissed him, again dry-lipped, firmly. June looked at Marie, and smiling a little, said, "You're too far away to reach him, so I'll kiss him for you." June kissed Garrett a second time, dry, firm.

Marie looked arrows at June.

Garrett sat dumbfounded.

June took the reins from Garrett. "All right, Lady, let's go for that spin."

"Hey," Garrett cried. "I never let nobody drive her."

"Never?"

"Never!"

Lady took over matters the next couple of seconds. She hadn't liked the foreign touch on her reins either. She broke into a gallop and rounded the next corner so fast the buggy lurched far over on two wheels. They didn't quite tip over.

Garrett grabbed the lines back and hauled Lady up short. It took him but a moment to have Lady stroking along at a decent pace again.

There wasn't much said for a while. They drove up and down the usual streets. Bells on Lady's bridle jingled merrily. Celluloid rings on Lady's checkrein gleamed white and scarlet in the pale light of the street lamps. Garrett was proud of the two silver bobs beside him, even if Marie's being along did cramp his style a little.

After a time Garrett smiled to himself. He'd figured something out. June's kiss in Marie's behalf had been drier and less firm than her kiss in her own behalf. Despite herself June had let him know that she was a little jealous of Marie, maybe even a little angry at Marie for letting him see how much she liked him. Marie had a crush on him all right. Hmm. He was making headway, after all. "Take your time," he counseled himself, "take your time, boy. Pretty soon the plums will be ripe and then they'll fall off on their own accord."

After an hour of gallivanting up and down the dusty streets of Bonnie, waving at friends, calling out greetings, Garrett took the Memling girls home.

Through the rest of October, and all through November, Garrett stayed away from June. He left the field wide open for the other boys at church. He made up his mind he was not going to ask her for

34

another date until she sought out his eyes at church or at Young People's. If she liked him, gol-darn, she could show it a little. Chase a woman too much and you found yourself married to a crab. The heck with that noise. Look at what happened to poor Barry Simmons when he married sister Ade. Barry had to leave Ade for a while to find out if he could still pee without having to squat like a woman.

The other boys in church were quick to sense that Garrett was laying off June for the time being. They pestered her to death, especially the big red-nosed Tamming boys. After about a month, she relented a little, and she and Marie accepted a couple of dates. By Christmas Day the word around town was that June was an iceberg while little Marie was a hotbox. The boys said June was probably going to wind up an old maid clerk for her father, while Marie as sure as sunrise was going to have a bad end. The only ones Marie was offish with were the Tamming boys.

New Year's Eve there was a party at cousin Slim John's, a square skip shindig. Alfred Alfredson came over to play the accordion, though he came without his wife Ada's permission. Ada was dead set against dances. It was against her religion. But Alf came anyway. He was the only really good player and square dance caller the Little Christian Churchers had. The great Crimp Wickett was a Congregationalist, so he couldn't very well be invited. The minister, Domeny Tiller, knew he had to allow his bunch a fling or two, and he always held off on his yearly "Sins of the Flesh" sermon until after New Year's Day.

Garrett decided to go. It was only a mile away, north over the back road, an easy three-minute drive with Lady. There just might be fun. Besides, he liked Slim John. Cousin Slim John was one of the taller Englekings, son of Alfred Engleking over in Sioux County. Slim John was full of the dickens and one heckuva first baseman. About the only thing Garrett had against Slim John was that he batted cross-handed.

Slim John's yard was lit up all around with lanterns hung in the trees. The two inches of fluff snow on the ground shone like freshly spilled maple sugar. The air was soft and even the loudest voices had a gentle cast about them.

The usual bunch from church was there: the Pipp boys and girls, the Fabers, the Ettens, the Coopers, the Lemons, even the Tamming boys, and of course some of Garrett's own brothers and sisters, the Englekings.

The Memling girls came late. And they came alone, no dates. Their folks were friends with the Fabers across the road, and so while the Memling elders were to visit with the Faber elders, the girls June and Marie walked over for the square skip.

Coffee and cake was served the whole evening long, and out in the milkshed there was some home-brew beer for the hairy boys. Alf and Fat John each brought a tubful of their own brew, the best around. Both Alf and Fat John used family recipes taken along from the Old Country, Alf from West Fries-land and Fat John from East Friesland. Neither beer ever had settlings in the bottom of the bottle. Uncap the bottle, pop! and there you had it, a light amber stream never darker than rain water, forming a last-ing head of fine-bubbled foam.

The cream-colored countryhouse was packed. Every kerosene and gas lamp Matilda had on hand blazed away. The square skip was held in the living room, with the furniture pushed back into the par-lor. Alf sat playing and calling partway up the stairs to the second floor. The kitchen was always jammed with those resting between dances, drinking coffee. A bright glossy calendar from the First National Bank of Bonnie showed the day on one wall while the framed portrait of Great John Engleking stared everyone right in the eye with Old Country disap-proval from the other wall. Great John was the family god and hero—he had once defied Bismarck and as Baron of a district known as Lengen in East Friesland had forthwith given up all his lands and

rights and escaped across the Dollert into West Friesland with his wife Adelheid and three children, sons
Big John and Alfred and daughter Alberta.

The square skip was stiffish at first, though long-
legged Alf called and played well right off. It took
the Little Christian Churchers a while to unwind.
But by eleven o'clock the coffee had spiced up the
girls and the homebrew in the milkshed had charged
up the boys. Then the dolls began to dance. Even
pregnant Matilda, Slim John's wife, took a few turns.

Drinking, watching, Garrett noted that June
partnered up most often with Bill Tamming. Bill in
his big rough way bounced June around as though
he were trying to shock a bundle of light oats. Oddly
enough Bill's roughness protected June from the hard
bones of the other boys, mostly because they knew
they'd get bested if it came to a game of bumping
butts.

Garrett finished yet another mug of beer, then
coolly, between numbers, went over and asked June
for the next skip. He did it right in front of Bill
Tamming.

June gave Garrett an appraisive blue look.
"What's Alf gonna play next?"

"Our own special number. 'Skip to My Lou.'"

June almost giggled. She appreciated his quick-
ness making that up. "All right. Do you mind, Bill?"

"You goddam right I mind!" Bill Tamming

roared, tipping back his sloping forehead, getting set to fight. "You're my gal tonight, I say."

June froze.

Almost everybody else stiffened too.

Highpockets Alf the accordion player got to his feet and called out, "Here now, boys, here!"

Slim John promptly emerged from the kitchen with a stove poker. "There'll be no monkeyshines in my house, boys! Garrett, what's the trouble?"

Garrett was smiling coolly. He was ready to take on Bill, big nose and all, and they would find out once and for all who was king in the Little Rock valley.

It was June who smoothed down ruffled feathers. "Bill seems to think he had a date with me tonight. And Garrett seems to want the next skip because the next number is gonna be our song. Well, if Bill wants a date with me, he can have it, and if Garrett wants this next number with me, he can have that."

Bill Tamming let down his rooster comb a little upon that and, smirking some in victory, let Garrett have June for the next skip.

Alf relaxed, and began to wrestle with the squeezebox again. Soon the quarrel was forgotten.

A half hour later everybody rang out the old year and sang in the new. There was a shout and a kiss and a high old skip at the corners.

Garrett managed to dance with June one more time. He got Alf to repeat "Skip to My Lou" around two o'clock. By this time June had come alive as he had never seen her before. Her eyes sheened a high blue and spots as red as eagle flowers showed on her pale cheeks.

June and Garrett sang together in turn:

> *Mother won't let me.*
> *Not even one?*
> *Mother won't let me.*
> *Not even one?*
> *Skip to my Lou my darling.*
>
> *It's two o'clock in the morning.*
> *Goodness gracious we must go,*
> *Mother and dad will worry so.*
> *I'll be glad to take you home*
> *In my great big sleigh.*
> *See you tomorrow,*
> *Skip to my Lou my darling.*

June kept her distance through all the turns, doing with Garrett just as she'd done with Bill Tamming.

"Darn her," Garrett thought, "she knows she's meant for me, that sooner or later she'll have to own up to it."

40

Then Garrett caught her just right in a dark corner behind the nickel hard-coal burner. She couldn't escape him, and for one fleeting moment it seemed to him she didn't try. He socked his groin into her lap, right against the bone, hard. The music beat three more times and on the fourth beat he went to sock her again. This time she arched her butt away from him, and he almost lost his balance.

June smiled. "Sometimes you're almost as rough as Bill."

After that number everybody went home.

A week went by.

All of a sudden Garrett caught pneumonia and almost died from it.

His brothers and sisters sat up with him by turns, and one night they were sure he was a goner. He was out of his head and kept talking about that bad man in a dark corner. They thought he was talking about Death, maybe even Satan. They called Domeny Tiller and he came and prayed over Garrett.

Garrett recovered slowly.

Dr. Fairlamb told him to take it easy for at least sixty days. "Loaf, if you wanna live," he said.

"And if I don't?"

"You'll have a relapse."

Garrett smiled weakly. "Looks like June is going to have to wait some more."

41

"Who?"

"As if she cared."

But June did care. It was hardly her place to take turns with the family sitting up with Garrett nights, since she and Garrett couldn't as yet be considered going together. Yet she thought about him night and day, and wondered what kind of get-well gift she could send him. She felt a little guilty about him getting sick. Had she been nicer to him maybe he would have done things a little differently and so have escaped the pneumonia. However, God's will.

One day in March she heard Garrett favored johnnycake. That gave her an idea. She baked a beauty, gold crust and gold heart. She wrapped the warm johnnycake in waxpaper and got her lank father to drive her out to the Engleking farm. Garrett was taking the sun on the cement stoop on the east side of the house when they drove up, and he took the waxpaper package from her himself. She saw how wan he looked, peaked, though his eyes twinkled as blue as ever, and his pompadour had a healthy straw color. His face opened when he saw what was in the package.

"Ma," Garrett called over his shoulder into the house, "Mem, put on the coffee pot."

"What do you think," a sharp woman's voice scolded from within, "that we're all without manners here?"

42

"No no, don't bother," June said. "Thanks anyway, but Pa's got to get back to the store. Some other time."

"Ma won't like that," Garrett said.

"I just wanted to bring this over, that's all. Quick like. You see, Pa just had time to bring this out. He's got to hurry back to the store. You know how Marie is clerking."

"Some other time for sure then? Promise?"

"Promise."

Garrett had some coffee anyway, along with half the pan of johnnycake. With melted fat and syrup the cornbread went down better than homemade ice cream.

Later that day he felt so full of pep he called June on the country line. "A couple more johnnycakes like that," he laughed, "and I'll take on even Wild Bill Tamming one-handed."

June managed to bring him two johnnycakes a week for a month. By the middle of April Dr. Fairlamb told Garrett he could pull his full weight on the farm again.

Garrett also began to date June steady.

The first Sunday they drove around and saw the sights, and talked and laughed together like old married folks. They didn't kiss.

The second Sunday it was different. And both knew it was different. It was in the air even. The

43

lilacs were out. So were the plums. The moonlight was heavy with the perfumes of newly burst blossoms.

"Shall we see who's all spooning who along Lovers' Lane?"

"Where is your secret place?" June asked instead. She was wearing a blue ribbon in her silver bob. "The little Garden of Eden you once wanted to show me."

A tremble moved through Garrett. "You mean, my place?"

"Yes."

The shaking in his limbs made it hard for him to see for a second. June really was another June that night all right. He had the funny feeling that while he might be trembling she was boiling. "All right," he said. "I've never showed it to anybody else. Hup, Lady."

Lady first thought he meant for them to go home, and headed east.

"No, no, girl." Gently Garrett pulled her around and pointed her nose west.

They drove under the Cannonball trestle, rolled past a patch of eagle flowers, rumbled across the plank bridge over the Big Rock River, and climbed the curving road up the hill. Right next to the entrance to the Bonnie Cemetery was a gate into a field. They found it open and drove through. They rolled north along the fence. The field had just been plowed and under the silver moon the raw earth looked like a flow of endless ribbons of syrupy tar. The faint trail along the fence soon ran into an alfalfa field. The alfalfa was up, a soft sprouting green resembling a thick carpet of tender onion sets.

Chokecherries grew along the line fence. Lady snorted at the chokecherry brush as if to suggest a coyote or a wolf might lie covert there.

At the quarter section line Garrett pulled up. "Whoa, girl."

Lady, stopping, looked around, curving her head for a peek at Garrett and June. Then, whinnying, she tried to reach down and graze. The grass under the line fence was already a foot high. It was so rich it had the succulent color of wild sorrel.

Garrett stepped down and unhooked Lady's checkrein so she could graze.

June said, "I don't see anything."

Garrett held out his hand. "Come." He helped her down from the buggy. "I'll show you."

"Is it far?"

"Come." He picked June up and with an easy swinging motion lifted her over the fence and set her down in the pasture on the other side. With an equally light swing, a hand on a fence post, he vaulted up and over and stood beside her.

He led her across the soft grass until they came

45

to a mound on the very edge of the hill. He took her elbow and helped her mount it.

She looked around wonderingly.

Garrett said, "The old codgers around here say this is an old Indian mound we're standing on."

"It is?" She pointed toward the lights of Bonnie glimmering across the river. "You can see town from here. Just as clear."

"Sometimes I like to come here alone and sit and smoke my pipe."

"It's kind of like a high pulpit in a big church."

"A high bandstand sort of."

"With thousands of stars for lights."

"And thousands of dandelions for candles."

They stood very still together. She was wearing a light blue dress and in the moonlight it made her hair more richly silver. He was wearing his dark blue serge suit, and in the same light it made his pompadour more richly golden.

They stood trembling together.

Then he put his arms around her and kissed her, and she put her arms around him and kissed him back. She let out a groan as she swung the bone in her lap hard against his groin. She hugged him.

They more fell to the ground than slipped. The new grass was soft. It smelled of clover. It smelled of well-sunned earth.

They hugged and hugged each other.

He had never touched a girl between the legs before. He trembled and shook. He fumbled his hand under her dress and wept tears of joy as he did it. My God, how soft her legs were. And she wasn't wearing bloomers either, like his sisters usually did. The flat of his hand brushed over a soft mound of hair, and first her legs opened, and she groaned, and then her legs closed, and she groaned.

"Girl, girl," he said, "lady, lady."

"I don't know what you do, Garrett," she whimpered softly, "I've never done it before."

"I ain't neither."

"But I don't know if I can wait any longer like the church says we must."

"I don't neither."

"Oh, Garrett."

"Girl."

He rested his hand on her soft mound of hair. The soft mound seemed to swell under his hand. He pressed down on it, firmly yet softly a few times. She pressed up in response each time. She moaned and twisted in his arms. He dropped a finger into the mound of hair and found the moist cleft. She cried out, and her legs closed like a pair of suddenly shut scissors. She grabbed his hand and held it away, then took his hand and put it back. She let her legs open again. When his finger found the cleft once more she held his hand away again.

"Garrett."

"Girl."

She opened her dress and bared her breasts to the moon. "Kiss them first," she said, "before you touch them with your hand." Her breasts lay upon her like a pair of white harvest apples, halved. "Kiss them, Garrett."

Violently trembling he reached down with his lips and touched her breasts. They quivered under his lips from all his trembling. And she trembled. He kissed them. Without thinking he suckled them a moment. She took hold of one of them and pressed it into his mouth.

"Garrett."

He thought: "They may look like apples but they really taste more like peaches. Ripe."

Slowly he got control of his trembling. He was so hard with love for her he thought he would burst. He kissed her breasts again and again. Then his hand went back to the mound of hair and found the cleft again. After a moment her lips parted under his.

"Oh, Garrett," she whispered hoarsely, "you don't have to worry about the maidenhead. I broke it myself once."

"My girl."

As in a slowly turning dream he opened his trousers and slid them down and mounted her. She had hold of him then and was helping him in before he himself thought of doing it. She was wild. She was more than making up for all those times she'd been cool to him. It went in wonderfully and they were doing it, doing it, and then before they knew it he almost fainted and she almost fainted, and then both began to gasp for what seemed their last breath on earth together.

She was all milk and wild roses. His face lay in her hair. The touch of her hair on his face was like the touch of spiderweb threads across his eyes. He lay in her valley of love and on her round belly a long time. From somewhere came the smell of freshly separated cream.

He was about to slide off and lie in the grass beside her and muse about their guilt together, when she moved ever so little, and in an instant he was once again so hard with love he almost burst. Once more they were making love, harsher and more frantic, and this time more knowing, anticipating what the other would do and what the other wanted, and very shortly both began to gasp through a second sweet fainting together.

The moon moved across the night.

June's blue ribbon lay slipped off to one side and her bob was spread upon the grass like poured silver. He cupped the back of her head in both his hands, and rested his body mostly on his elbows. His elbows rested in the grass on either side of her hips. He hung

49

lightly over her except where they touched at their secret places. He loved her.

"You're my girl now, June. I love you."

"I love you, Garrett." She cradled him in her arms and legs.

"Will you marry me, girl?"

"Oh, Garrett, I'm just sixteen. And you're just eighteen. We're too young. We'd never get our parents' permission."

"Elope with me then, June. I can't wait now."

"Garrett."

"I've got a little money saved up from picking corn. Pa says he'll give me a team of horses and a plow when I get married. And Ma says she'll give me some laying hens and a cow. The horse and buggy are already mine."

"I worry about my pa so, with only that dumb Marie to help him."

"What about your other sisters? Ain't one of them about ready to take your place? Alice, say? She's twelve, ain't she? She's a deadringer for you already."

"Pa don't think so."

Garrett had to be careful about what he said next. "You've got a good pa, June. I like him. But he's got to see that his children will finally grow up. Like he once did. That you're about ready to have your own family soon."

50

"We've still got to ask him for permission. We're not of age, Garrett."

"I averaged a hundred thirty-five bushel at Frank Westings last fall. Earned a lot of money. Broke the record twice and got five cents a bushel."

Cool air touched her white legs. She closed them under him.

"Here," he said, "let me . . ." He released himself gently from her and slid to one side. He drew her dress down. While she closed her dress he buttoned up his trousers. Then he put his arms around her from the side and threw a warm leg over her. She snuggled close. She shivered, once, and cuddled even closer.

"Will you farm then?" she asked after a time.

"I been thinking. You see, Bonnie could use a good wellman and plumber. After Old Aitchison died we ain't had nobody. Have to call all the way to Rock Falls when your pump breaks down."

She stirred languorously in his arms. "You'll have a shop in town then."

"I guess so."

"Then I could help Pa Saturdays. Still."

"What about Alice by then?"

"I'm afraid Pa won't think she's old enough for quite a while."

"Shall I talk to your pa and ma about us? A lot

of young folks get married before they're of age. They get the folks' consent."

"I hope I don't get a baby right away."

"You don't always get a baby every time you do it."

"That would be awful. Ma would never get over it. The shame. And Pa, he might still give me a licking. He can, you know, legally, until I'm eighteen."

"He don't look like a licker to me. He's so easy in his ways when you talk to him."

"He's that all right, yes. But did you ever notice he never gives credit to nobody? You don't know him like I do." She moved in his arms. "Yes, my pa might lick me all right if I got a baby."

"After we're married too?"

"No, I mean, before we got married. Without his permission."

"We'll be all right if we get married in a couple of weeks. Even with tonight."

Silence.

"June?"

Suddenly she sat up. "I don't think I can, Garrett. Not right away. And I shouldn't've done it with you tonight. But I finally just couldn't help myself." She took his round warm face in her slim hands. "Garrett, why do you think I held off from you all this time? There was a reason, you know. When I knew from that time when I looked at you in the store that I had to have you some day."

"Don't you love me?"

"Of course I love you, Silly."

"But?"

"I can't let Pa run that store alone. I've got to help him until I'm at least eighteen."

"That's not the real reason now, is it?"

"It is. It is."

"Oh, come now."

"Pa's awful jealous of his girls. Awful jealous."

"So?"

"He wants the best for his girls. You know. He wants for them to grow up good Christian girls."

"He's forgot he was young himself once."

Stillness.

"Ask him sometime if he has the right to throw the first stone."

"Garrett!"

"Well, by gol, I will if you won't."

"Garrett."

Garrett thought: "I'll give her a little time."

Then he took her home.

Garrett saw her three times a week for a while: Wednesday night after the store closed, Saturday night after the store closed, and Sunday night after Young People's Catechism. All through May, June and July, they went each time to their secret place on

53

the high hill west of town and made love. Each time June was wild to have him and each time too June had some reason with which to stall him about their getting married.

Around the first of August she suddenly wouldn't let him anymore.

At first he thought it was because she maybe was going to have a baby. He was scared. He didn't sleep much for a couple of weeks.

In September he finally dared to ask her.

"No," she said. "I just thought it would be better for us if we didn't do it any more until we got married."

"Until when?"

Silence.

"June, I'm going crazy this way. You let me get started and now I can't stop."

"Poor Garrett, I know."

"Please, let's go see your pa and ma and tell them we want to get married."

"Let's wait. Make sure this is the real thing."

"June!"

Stillness.

"Because I can't stand it this way. It isn't good for the man if you first let him for a while and then shut him off. It's onnatural."

"Winter is almost here. Let's see again in the spring."

54

That night Garrett cursed all the way home.

Everybody in church and everybody uptown began to wonder about them. Garrett began to wonder himself sometimes. Sometimes he found it hard to recall those urgent and feverish and lustful nights they'd once had together on the Indian mound.

They were cool to each other at Christmas time.

New Year's Eve they went to a square skip and, yes, he skipped with her. But he didn't care to sock his groin into her lap again in the dark corners. And she just barely permitted him a dry kiss when he took her home.

In January and February, during the cold snaps and the worst of the winter's blizzards, they hardly saw each other.

In March he finally broke away from his pa and ma, and set up shop on Main Street as a plumber and wellman, with a side line of hardware merchandise to sell on Wednesday and Saturday nights. Big John Engleking approved of the move, and so did Ma Engleking, and instead of giving him a team of horses and a plow, and chickens and a cow, as they'd done with their other boys, they bought out the old Aitchison store with all the fixtures and deeded it over to him. That was to be Garrett's full inheritance and no more.

Garrett's new store was on the same side of the street as the Memling Mercantile, up the block near the town tennis courts. The Post Office was across the street, on the south side. Sometimes he met June there, getting the mail before he went out on a call. He'd walk over from his shop, and she from her father's store, and they'd talk a while.

In April they were back to seeing each other once a week, on Sunday nights.

All of a sudden in May she wondered aloud about their secret place on the hills west of town.

Garrett broke out in one of the worst cases of trembles he ever had. "You mean, our Indian mound?"

"Yes."

All the way out there, with Lady going like the wind, past the eagle flowers and the wild bullberries, over the rumbling plank bridge, up past the cemetery gate, June clung to him closer and closer, and ardent, so that when he at last swung her over the line fence, she ran skipping across the pasture to their mound.

"Garrett, Garrett," she cried. "It's been so long I can hardly wait."

He was so engorged he had trouble running.

They fell on the grass. She helped him put his hands in all the right places. She seemed to be seething inside. She made a noise a little like a kettle of boiling water. "Hurry," she whispered fiercely, "hurry." Other times she'd been the one to want to dally a little before she'd let him climb the mount of love. Not this time. "Slowpoke," she cried. "Such a slowpoke."

"I'll show you," he said. And did.

They were rough together. Wild. Crazy. And when they finally swooned away together again it was like they'd had an epileptic fit. Her blue ribbon slid off onto the grass. Her silver hair lay spread like a spiderweb heavy with dew.

Before they did it a second time she made him suckle her breasts.

They were all of a seethe through May and June and July. Then in August, just as before, she cooled off.

It took him a while to understand this. In the gossip at his hardware store he heard an odd thing. A Swede named Ekebo claimed he'd once married a Laplander, a blond who'd do it only in the spring. She was dead now. "They're like the deer up there," Swede Ekebo said. "Or like the Eskimo. Once a year they screw night and day for a solid month, in May it is, and then for the rest of the year they're like a bunch of spayed dogs together. Nothing."

This time, though, there was another reason why June was offish in August.

She told him in September.

They were riding home from Catechism in his buggy. As he pulled up to let her off at her home, she said, "Wait. I don't want to go in just yet. Drive on a little."

Garrett gave her a wondering look. "Shall we take a little spin up to our mound?"

"Drive."

Garrett pulled Lady around, and soon they were rolling under the Cannonball trestle and over the rumbling bridge and up the hill. As they approached their secret lane next to the entrance to the cemetery, June reached out a hand and pulled on Lady's right rein. Lady veered and clip-clopped under the overhead grillwork of the cemetery gate.

"What the dickens?" Garrett exclaimed. "Not in here. Really now. This is the place for the dead."

"It's where I belong," she said.

Garrett hauled up on Lady, hard, and stopped her. "June! What's the matter with you? You nuts or something?"

"Garrett, I'm going to have a baby."

He stared at her. Even in the vague dark he could make out what looked like a small bat hanging under each of her eyes. "So that's it."

"Garrett, what do we do now?"

"Get married, of course. I was right in the first place."

"Garrett, I can't. Pa and Ma'll die of shame if we get married before we're of age."

Garrett swore. "The hell with them then. It's our

baby, not theirs, and we've got to live our own life, not theirs."

"It's not that easy."

"Why not? We'll first drive up to Rock Falls tomorrow and get our license."

"Without their permission?"

"I'm going to get that license myself then. Tomorrow. Alone. Even if I have to lie about our age."

"Garrett, ain't you worried what your pa will think?"

"Pa will say to go ahead. So will Ma. They like you. Besides, what can they do if they don't like the idea? They've already given me my inheritance."

"Oh."

"Come on. Let's go see your folks and tell 'em. And get it over with. Then tomorrow we'll get our license. Before it's too late. We still got time to claim it's an early baby, hain't we?"

"Garrett." She wept. "I just can't." She wept. "I just can't." Then she broke down completely. She cried so hard even Lady arched her head around to see what the noise was about.

Garrett was more than moved. He was scared. "All right, girl. We'll talk about it later. We've got time."

"Garrett, why did we have to do it in the first place. I can't understand it."

"Ha. Why does oats grow in the spring? Or birds

59

make nests? Or rabbits have little rabbits in the meadow? God's will."

"And then even after we've told our parents, there's still the church board to face."

"What about it?"

"Hoo. I'd rather face the United States Supreme Court than those hard-faced men."

"We'll see to that when we get there."

He took her home.

They went around and around on the same subject. He just couldn't get her to agree to tell their parents.

She'd heard that heavy lifting sometimes caused miscarriages. She lifted boxes at the store that not even her pa would tackle.

No luck. Slowly her sweet belly began to swell.

Again Garrett urged her to elope with him. They'd run off to South Dakota.

No.

By Thanksgiving even Garrett began to have bats hanging under his eyes.

At Christmas, Big John Engleking took Garrett aside. It was at Garrett's store. Big John was tall and burly and he had a huge bay window. Yet for all his weight he could walk as supple as a lean young man. He had fierce gray eyes and an impressive gray spade beard.

"Garrett, boy, what's eating you lately?"

"Nothing."

"Something's wrong, son. It ain't your business, is it?"

"No."

"I heard you're giving out too much credit."

"I got some outstanding, yes."

"How much?"

"Oh, about a third."

"Who to?"

"Mostly our church people."

Big John let out a roar like that of a gored bull. "Dammit, boy, never give credit to your own church people. They're the worst."

"They look all right to me."

"Boy, listen. You've got to be tough with people in business. Business is the guts of a country and you know you never take a chance with the guts of a person. Look at John Memling. Starting from nothing he's worked himself up into a pretty good thing here in Bonnie. Because he don't give credit, that's why."

"He can run his business his way and I can run my business my way, I say."

"Boy, boy. You're too soft. You've got to be hard in business. Hard. Or you'll go bankrupt as sure as the moon goes backwards. Be hard."

Garrett knew what the old man meant all right. Garrett even had trouble being hard with June, making her tell her pa and ma.

"You sure it ain't your business eating you?"

"No."

"What about you and June then? Everything all right there?" Big John drilled a knowing look into Garrett. "Ain't you two fixing to get married pretty soon?"

"June won't be of age until the fourth of April."

"Haw. Me and your ma didn't wait for a little thing like that."

"That's what I told June."

"So it's that then, eh?"

"Well, not exactly. She likes me all right, I guess."

"What is it then?"

"Not now, Pa. I'll tell you sometime later."

New Year came. June took to wearing a corset.

Valentine's Day came. June laced the corset tight and close.

March came in like a lamb. June wouldn't let the corset out as much as a quarter of an inch. And she suddenly looked a fright. The way she walked she looked like she was about to come down with paralysis.

"June," Garrett begged, "let's tell them."

"No."

"You're as pale as a ghost, girl."

She shook her head.

"This is crazy. What are you going to do when it's born? They're sure to know then, you know."

"No."

"You going to hide it in the weeds somewhere? Like that woman in the Bible did with the baby Moses?"

"I'm not going to have the baby until after the next fourth of April. Then we can get a license without their permission. Sometimes there can be such a thing as a long-term pregnancy."

Garrett was wild. "Listen! Even if the baby is born right after we're married they're going to talk."

"It's going to be the way I say."

On the first day of spring, the twenty-second of March, Garrett, looking out of his shop window, saw June fall down as she was crossing the street on the way to the Post Office.

Garrett was beside her in a couple of leaps. When he picked her up, he saw she was bleeding down one leg. Quickly, before a crowd gathered, he ran with her up the street and stormed into Dr. Fairlamb's office. Garrett's face was as white as fresh snow.

Dr. Fairlamb took one look and ordered Garrett to bring her straight into the operating room. Then he pushed Garrett out.

An hour later, Garrett got the news. June had her baby all right. Their baby. A dead baby. Green.

Doc said it'd probably been dead for some time. Because all of June's insides were infected with gangrene.

63

Two hours later, June was dead.

And four days later, Garrett was in a hospital. He'd slipped while fixing a windmill and had broken his right arm and cracked some ribs.

"Darling June Memling, she died of the green gangrene."...

3

Garrett clopped out his pipe, put away the blue ribbon, rehooked Lady's checkrein, and climbed back into his buggy.

Lady liked the luscious grasses between the graves, and she resented having to leave the cemetery. She held her chestnut neck curved against him until they crossed the plank bridge below.

In Bonnie, Garrett tied Lady up to a hitching post behind Rexroth's. He carried in Ada Alfredson's eggs and got some groceries for her: a sack of flour, some dried prunes, a box of oatmeal, a box of cornmeal, a box of raisins, and a packet of needles.

65

Big Bill Tamming was lazing around in the back of the store, sprawled out on some sacks of sugar, a cigar in his mouth. Big Bill gave Garrett a slow, sly smile.

"Say, Garrett, I hear the Prince of Wales is coming through this part of the country this summer. Visiting America. I suppose you'll be putting him up for a couple of weeks, hah, seeing he's probably your cousin?"

"You betcha."

"I hear the Prince of Wales is quite a fellow with the girls. Ain't you afraid he'll beat your time with Laura Pipp?"

"If he can do it, he's welcome to her."

"Pretty sure of yourself, aincha?"

"You tell'm."

Big Bill sneered. "Well, if the Prince of Wales did diddle her, you wouldn't know the difference in the kid anyway, bein' as how you two are deadringers for each other. Everybody says."

"Just like you're a deadringer for some wolves I know." Garrett laughed. "One of these days you're going to get your ass full of prickles."

"How so?"

"Because I'm gonna take a club to you someday and scare you backwards into them wild plums by the bridge there."

Big Bill swelled a deep red.

66

Garrett thought: "Yeh, and if he knew about Laura, he'd swell up a mad red."

Garrett took the north road out of town and headed east. The cemetery grass had given Lady a lot of run and she ate up the miles. Coming over the third roll of prairie, Garrett's eye instinctively sought out the Pipp place. Yep. There was the light in the kitchen. The folks were still up. And Laura was probably out in the seat swing waiting for him.

Garrett's eye next sought out the back pasture of the Young place across the Little Rock River. It was the secret place where he and Laura had first spooned together. With narrowed eyes he thought he could make out the line fence where it had happened that first time.

. . . Garrett was picking corn for Alf on the north forty near the line fence. It was late in the afternoon, October. Field spiders were loosing silk lines to catch the last of the fall flies. Garrett finished his fifth time across the field and turned his grays around to start back for the next two rows. Just as he was about to take a sip from a burlap-wrapped water jug, he heard a girl calling up the cows. It was Laura Pipp.

Garrett had met eyes with Laura in church a couple of times. He knew she had a slight crush on him. But he hadn't done anything about it because of what had happened with him and June. He had sworn off women. It had been hard sometimes, and very lonesome, but he had done it. One of the reasons he'd taken the job with Alf and Ada was to make sure that he would stay away from the girls. Alf's honesty and Ada's Christian heart would help him toe the line. The way Ada could talk sometimes, very quietly, yet with a warm full heart, why! not even the Devil himself would have dared to fool around with girls while living with her. Long-geared Alf didn't know how lucky he was.

Garrett knew Laura was working for Sam Young's. Old Drewes Pipp already had the corn out, mostly because he made his girls help his boys during corn picking. When Sam Young went over to ask for Laura to help while his wife had her baby, Old Drewes Pipp let her go. Sam Young particularly wanted Laura because she was handy in the yard. He wanted her not only to help in the house but also to do chores for him while he got out the rest of his corn.

Garrett was sure Laura had seen him before he'd seen her. That was why she was calling the cows a little extra loud.

He couldn't help but admire Laura's physique as she approached. She was a real chunk of a girl. Like a short-coupled cow pony. Stubby and quick. And she looked pretty good, too, dressed up in a man's clothes. Her Sunday dress didn't do too well by her, mostly because styles those days favored the skinny girl.

Garrett finished his drink and put the jug back. A spider thread tickled his cheek. He rubbed the spot on his plain sleeve.

A breeze rustled through the standing corn.

The grays had their bellies full at last. They stood on three legs, loose-lipped, drooling, waiting for him to begin picking again.

"Hi there, handsome," Laura finally called.

"Hi there yourself, beauty."

Laura was about to say something more, when suddenly two yearling Frisian heifers decided they didn't want to go home with the rest of the cows. There was still some luscious grass growing in Fool's Gold Gully, while at home there was only an old dirty strawpile butt to eat. With a girlish bellow and a tail-high caper, the black-and-white heifers wheeled and tried to streak past Laura.

The corner of Laura's eye caught the movement. Wheeling on a toe, away Laura went after the flying heifers. Like a smart cow pony she immediately made a shortcut for the fence to head them off. Running like a very fast fat man, she beat the heifers there. The surprised heifers planted down all four feet and came to a skidding stop in the greasy grass. Their eyes came out like big glowing daisies. They couldn't believe it. Laura skidded to a stop herself, and in almost the same motion she picked up a dried horse biscuit and let fly. Garrett was astounded to see how well she could throw. She had the peg of a catcher. She hit the nearest heifer between the eyes, smack on its white forehead. That did it. Both heifers turned tail and rejoined the rest of the herd.

"Whew!" Laura wiped her hand on her pant leg. "Sam warned me about them frisky heifers. He was right."

Garrett leaned a hand on the rear wheel of his wagon. "Why bring them home?"

"Sam says there's wolves around. He's worried they might get one of his heifers some night."

Garrett smiled to himself. "Guess there is some wolves around all right. I know of at least one myself."

"I see you taking a drink. Got any left? I'm thirsty after that run."

"Sure thing."

Garrett helped her through the fence, holding the barbwires apart. The cows slowly one by one vanished over the edge of the hill in the direction of the Young farmyard.

Garrett and Laura climbed up the side of the wagon together. The wagon box was heaping full of gold corn. To get the next two rows on Garrett would have to add a sideboard. Garrett dug out the water jug where he'd stuck it up front and handed it to her. She pulled the cob cork and tilted the jug up on her crooked arm. She guggled herself a long pull.

Musky fermentive fumes rose from the freshly picked corn beside them. Garrett observed her soberly. What a handy chunk she was.

"Haaa," she said, letting the jug down at last. "Good. A burlap sack sure does keep it nice and cool."

"This time of the year it's never very hot."

"It has been nice this fall, hasn't it?"

"Wonderful for picking." Garrett smiled into her deepset black eyes. He noted that up close she had a perky nose. If it weren't for those thin lips—like a man's almost—she'd be good-looking. A beauty.

"Dry." She combed back her dark hair with her fingers. "And just cool enough so you don't work up much of a sweat no matter how fast you pick."

"When the spiders come out with their silk ropes you always can count on it being a good fall."

Laura laughed. She bounced her firm belly against the side of the green wagon. "I dreamt about them last night."

"How so?"

"It was like I was at a picnic. There was some foot races and every time I lined up and ran with the boys, these spiders would come along and tangle up my legs with their little silk ropes. I just couldn't run. Finally I cried myself awake."

71

"Funny. I've had dreams like that myself some-times."

"You mean with spider threads?"

"Well, not spider threads exactly. But about be-ing all tangled up. In baling wire. I'm trying to catch Lady so I can go to town, and yet I can't somehow, and so finally Lady comes up of herself and lets me put the bridle on her. Lets me slip the bit between her lips."

"That's like mine all right."

"Can't say I like that kind of a dream either."

Laura's quick black eyes spotted something in the wagon box. "Say, ain't that a red ear? Peeking out there?"

"When I find them now and then I throw 'em up front."

"Hey. I'm collecting red corn for Pa. He's start-ing up a new kind of corn and we're all out watching for them for him." Laura climbed onto the load. On all fours she scrambled across the corn and dug the red ear out. "What a beauty. Good dent. Deep kernel. Just the kind Pa wants."

"There's a couple more down in there some-where," Garrett said. "I'll find 'em for you." He climbed onto the load too.

Shoulder to shoulder they dug into the golden pile. A few ears still had leaves on and Garrett re-moved the leaves and threw them overboard. The corn leaves drifted slowly to the ground. Laura and Garrett found three more red ears.

"I think that's all," Garrett said. "I only remember picking four."

Laura hugged the red ears to herself. Brown hair trailed from their tips. The ears stuck out of her arms like they might be pointed breasts.

Laura gave him an intimate look. A soft catching laugh broke from her. Plainly she expected him to put a hand on her.

He did put a hand on her. A mittened hand on her thigh. And the Garrett Engleking he'd been a half hour ago, a hard-working hired hand with his mind set on paying off a deficiency judgment at the First National as well as remaining a warm friend of high-minded cousin Ada—that Garrett Engleking was suddenly a mere dirt wall giving way before a raging cloudburst. His ears roared. Violent trembles shook his belly. Quite automatically he undid his cornhook and took off his mittens.

Laura was willing. The moment he slipped his arm around her waist she groaned and leaned against him. Her eyes closed. She let the four red ears fall to one side.

Together Garrett and Laura fell backwards on the mounded load. Garrett's cap slipped off. His fallen pompadour was exactly the color of the gold corn. Garrett fumbled open her shirt and cupped her bare breasts. Her small breasts had the same feel as an overfull dog's udder, except that her nipples were fallen in a little. She didn't giggle. She was so hot for it she was dead serious. Her black bob bunched up around her face. He kissed her. He was surprised to find her kiss fleshy and moist despite her thin lips. When she puckered up the inner edges of her lips came out.

She panted. He panted.

When he put his hand between her legs she quickly helped him pull down her overalls and took one leg out. She opened her thighs for him. His wide hand caught her black brush full across. A fingertip felt live wet inner flesh, and the next moment, throbbing like a great fat horse's tongue, he was inside her. Four thrusts and the swoon was on him. But Laura wouldn't let him go. She was only just getting ready. She kept pumping her arch of bone against him. He just lay on her. Her frantic go-ups pleased him. A couple of times her sucking motion evoked after-spasms in him. She didn't say a word, but lips tight, eyes volving under closed lids, she pumped and gasped and pumped. Then a ratching purr started in her throat. The wet purr made him shiver with delight, and after a moment or two, still firm and long in her, another passage of desire rose in him, and this time, seizing her by the bare buttocks, he drew her hotly close and gave her all he had. Sweet was

74

the smell of freshly picked corn in his nostrils. She didn't seem to mind the hard lumpy corn under her back. Suddenly she had three wild spasms for his one. She more quivered against him than pumped against him. They cried out together at the same time.

They lay subsiding together.

Garrett expected to feel guilty. But to his great surprise he didn't at all. His conscience even seemed to be glad about it. It made him open his eyes a little. Either his Christian conscience had gone all to pieces, or he had been doing the wrong thing staying away from girls after June Memling's death.

Laura lay glowing in his arms.

Garrett liked Laura.

Presently Laura sighed, kissed him on his gold-red cheek, and said, "Guess I better bring the cows home the rest of the way." She laughed merrily. "That's what comes of chasing after two wild heifers." She rolled out from under him and put her clothes on. "Well, see you tomorrow, handsome."

Garrett also laughed as he pulled up his overall suspenders and slipped on his mittens and cornhook again. "Tomorrow then, my beauty?"

"Maybe."

"Promise?"

"We'll see."

"Promise?"

75

She laughed. "I can't promise to make them two heifers run away at the exact same spot. They may try it closer to the barn next time."

"Just get the cows like always," he said, "and I'll see to it that they run away at the right time."

It rained the next day. And it snowed the second day. They didn't get a chance to meet in the field again that week.

That Sunday, sitting across the aisle from her in church, meeting eyes with her, Garrett did some hard thinking about Laura Pipp. He found that he not only liked her, but that he liked her an awful lot. And he still didn't feel bad about having made love to her. In fact he began to see that what they'd done was a God-given right. So that night after Young People's, he asked her if he could take her home.

Laura was up in his buggy before he had the fur robe turned back for her on her side.

"Don't do anything I wouldn't do, Sis," Margaret Pipp, her sister, called from the sidewalk. Margaret gave them both a warm, wide laugh.

Allie Pipp her other sister called, "And don't forget Pa said me and Sherm was to have the parlor tonight."

Laura laughed. "We know of a better place than that old parlor."

"You betcha," Garrett said. "Out in the kitchen where Ma makes the hot chocalary."

Behind Margaret and Allie Pipp stood a quartet of sour-faced girls all in their late twenties. They were the Highmire girls and they had walked up and down between Main Street and the church for at least a decade still looking for their first date. It was plain to see the Highmire girls thought the Pipp girls plenty wild. And it was also plain to see they thought Garrett Engleking a dirty old fornicator, a devil incarnate.

Garrett wiggled his buggy whip until it gave off a low lacing whistle. "Why don't you Highmires make a play for the Tammings once? You could help each other be lonesome. Besides it'd be fun to speculate on the kind of pups we'd get out of such a match."

Lady had enough of all the flapping; she veered around and with a roll of her chestnut buttocks was off for the country.

Garrett and Laura didn't fool around that night though. Garrett had made up his mind beforehand that he was going to spend the evening having a sensible talk with a girl instead of the usual. Just to see. To his delight Laura was game. She seemed to anticipate his mood even before he was aware he had it. She wasn't so dumb. June was maybe smarter, and surely prettier, but June hadn't known how to go out of her way to please a man like Laura did. Laura was made to be the good wife, while June had always stood off to one side, a special breed.

Garrett and Laura discussed their Domeny and agreed that Reverend Tiller was a real card. They discussed Alf and Ada and agreed that that couple was among the best of the practicing Christians around. Laura asked Garrett if it were true the Englekings were distantly related to the Prince of Wales, and Garrett said he had heard such a story at a family reunion once, though Great John would never talk about it. "The Prince is probably some kind of shirttail relation of ours?" They both laughed at that.

"How old are you, Laura?"

"Seventeen."

"When was that?"

She started to laugh; checked herself. "You won't believe this, but it was that day last week when those two heifers tried to get past me."

"Oh."

"Best birthday present I ever had."

"No regrets then?"

"None."

"Even if Reverend Tiller should happen to preach on the Seventh Commandment?"

"Well, a little then, I suppose. But otherwise not. I've already asked God to forgive me. And I'm sure he has because my conscience don't bother me none."

"Same here. Sometimes I wonder if them preachers are right."

"That's what I think."

Christmas came with a tremendous snowstorm. The snow fell so thick, so fast, so heavy that many a family couldn't make it home following the afternoon church program.

The Sam Youngs got as far as the Pipp place and then gave up. From there they called Laura, who had stayed home with the baby, to let her know where they were.

Christmas was Garrett's day off at the Alfredsons and he had planned to pick Laura up in the evening to take her to a party at Slim John's. And while Sam and family couldn't make it home to Laura and baby, Garrett did.

Laura was overjoyed to see Garrett emerge out of the raging blizzard. She had been about to go out and do Sam's chores. She threw her arms around Garrett. "Handsome does as handsome is, I see."

"You all right here, girl?"

"I'm fine."

"How's the babe?"

"Fine."

Garrett stomped around on the green linoleum floor in the kitchen to get rid of the snow. "Tell you what."

"What?"

"Dig me out some of Sam's yard duds and I'll do the chores for you. While you cook us up a real old-fashioned country supper. That way you won't have to leave the baby alone in the house."

"We'll make believe we're an old married couple, hah."

"You betcha."

Sam's clothes were a little tight for him, but by leaving some of the buttons open, Garrett made them do. Laura lit a lantern for him and away Garrett went out into the storm again.

It took him two hours to get all the feeding and milking and separating done. He was exhausted when he came in. His face showed it. There was a strange blue like the color of skim milk over his cheeks.

He drew up a chair to the kitchen range and put his stocking feet up on the nickel railing. "Sam got any wine around?"

"I'll go see."

The wind jerked at the corners of the house.

Laura came back with a blue jug. "What's this smell like?"

Garrett took a sniff, and immediately color returned to his pale cheeks. "It's wine, all right. And how. Smells a little like it might be my favorite. Dandelion wine. The strongest and the best there is."

Both had some—Garrett a big glass full and Laura a small swallow in a cup.

Laura served him one of the best suppers ever: crisp fried potatoes, canned sausage, red cabbage, snap beans, hot tea and, best of all, warm johnnycake with maple syrup.

"That was lekker."

"I thought you'd like it."

"Now for a little snooze and I'm ready for the night."

Laura laughed a catching laugh. "I'll show you where you can lay down. But don't you fall asleep on me for the night. Too lonesome with that wind roaring up."

"Wonder what Slim John's going to do with all that ice cream he ordered for the party?"

Laura thickened around the eyes. "Too bad he don't live closer or we could've had a little party here of our own."

"Ha, you betcha."

He lay down on the couch in the living room and napped while Laura washed the dishes and changed the baby.

He woke up to the playing of "Beautiful Ohio" on Sam's phonograph.

Garrett lay listening to it until it was finished. "That's Ada's song. She's always playing it over t' Alf's."

"Sometimes I sing it to myself," Laura said. "It's one of my favorites too."

Garrett lay with his hands under his head. The glass kerosene lamp on the round center table burned low, casting a warm mellow light. The blizzard continued to moan under the eaves. Snow hung packed on the window panes outside. Thinking about cousin Ada and her song, thinking about the thing he had once done to June Memling, put him in a mood that was a far cry from the mood he'd been in a couple of months ago in that cornfield along the line fence.

Laura spotted the mood. "You wouldn't like another glass of Sam's dandelion wine?"

He stood up. "You know, I been thinking, bein' we're kind of man and wife here tonight, maybe we shouldn't do anything to ruin it for ourselves. You won't be eighteen anyway until next October."

Laura's face dropped. "I know."

He stretched to his full length, up on his toes. "I'll check all the stoves and then you better show me where I'm to sleep tonight."

"Welll . . ." Then she cut herself off short. "You can sleep in the Sam Youngs' bed, I suppose. It's down the end of the hall there. While I'll sleep in the front bedroom with the baby."

"Good."

That's what they did.

Around two in the morning the wind let up suddenly. The abrupt absence of its howling woke Garrett.

He lay a while, listening, then began to wonder if the Sam Youngs kept a thundermug under the bed. Because he had to go. When he finally saw he couldn't stall it off until morning, he got out of bed and on hands and knees felt around under the bed.

"Darn," he muttered. "Mrs. Young must've emptied it when she got up and left it in the privy to air out." With a hand to a knee, he got to his feet. "I'll have to go outdoors after all. Even if it is only to pee. Brrr, it'll be cold."

He slipped on his shoes, and in his long underwear, feeling his way down the hall as quietly as possible, finally made it outside. The snow was knee deep by the door, so he stepped only as far as the edge of the porch, and quietly, shivering, urinated into a snowdrift.

When he stepped back into the house his teeth were chattering like a battery of telegraph keys. He sought out the kitchen range but found only vague warmth in its stove lids. He moved on to the hard-coal burner. That was better. He stood beside its dim blue light a while, turning all sides of himself to its gentle warmth.

Chatters gone, he headed back for bed.

As he was about to pass Laura's room, he saw that the door was open and a light was on.

He glanced inside. Laura was busy doing something with the baby. Standing in her long white nightgown she looked strangely slim. The nightgown hung as much from the points of her stub breasts as it did from her sturdy shoulders.

"Anything the matter?"

Laura smiled at him over her shoulder. "Only a wet pants, is all."

He stood watching her.

She finished the diapering, put the dirty diaper in a white pail, then turned to go back to bed. She picked up her pillow and fluffed it a couple of times, put the pillow back, threw him a quick glance, and stopped.

They looked at each other, eyes glittering in the yellow light.

She moved first. She turned the night lamp down until it was almost out, then hopped into bed. But she didn't cover herself.

He stared at her.

"Garrett, be a devil for once."

Garrett's little fellow leaped and became a big boy almost on the instant. It made its way out of the front of the underwear on its own. He trembled in the doorway. At last, with a groan, eyes half-closed, he kicked off his shoes and went over and slid in beside her.

They threw their arms around each other and

hugged each other until their arms cracked in their shoulder sockets. It was so good to find a warm place in a bed with a sweetheart on a cold stormy night. Then both withdrew a little, and she slipped out of her nightgown, and he took off his long underwear; and without another word he put himself into her.

They did it four times before morning. Each time it was as if they were already doing it when they woke up. They'd do it, and fall asleep, and wake up and do it again. And that was the night when Laura got caught. . . .

4

Arriving on the Pipp yard, Garrett drove Lady straight for some deep grass behind the chicken house. He got down, undid Lady's checkrein so she could graze, then headed directly for the seat swing.

Laura was sitting on the far seat. In the darkness it seemed to him she already looked quite swollen with child. How could she expect to keep it hidden much longer? Unless, of course, she were to wear a tight corset. He shuddered.

"Hi," he said.

"Hi."

"Sorry I'm late." He stretched. "Ahhh. Had to pick up some groceries for Ada."

"I thought that was probably it."

He stood above her.

"Have a seat, why don't you?"

"Laura, I've made up my mind for us. Come, we're going in to tell your folks. And then we'll go over and tell my folks."

Laura shrank back in the dark. Her voice came out small. "No."

"I've already told Alf and Ada."

"You didn't."

"Yep. There's gonna be no more stalling around."

"No, Garrett."

"C'mon."

"I'm scared."

"Not me. Not any more I ain't."

"No."

Garrett wheeled on his heel anyway and started for the cream-colored Pipp house.

Laura jumped out of the seat swing and ran heavily after him. "No, Garrett, please. Pa'll kill me."

"Not in front of me, he won't. The little runt. I'll swat him down if he gets buzzy."

"Ma'll be out of her mind."

"It's really you who's going to be out of her mind, thinking you can hide it until God knows when."

"I want to try until I'm eighteen."

Garrett almost jumped out of his skin. He gnashed his teeth. "Then I suppose after you're married you're going to hold it back yet another nine months to make it all look proper and Christian?"

"Garrett."

"Nope. My mind is made up. Coming with me?"

"Hooo, Garrett."

Garrett took her by the arm and marched her straight for the front door.

"They may be in bed already," she said weakly.

"I saw a light in the back of the house."

They entered the darkened living room. A light shone through the half-opened door of the old folks' bedroom.

"Pa?" Garrett called. "Ma? Could we see you a minute?"

There was a rustle of sheets in the bedroom.

"Pa? Ma?"

Old Drewes Pipp spoke up. "Yes, son. What's the matter?"

"Me and Laura wanna see you a minute."

Some swift sharp whispering followed, mostly by Ma Pipp.

"Can't it wait until morning, son? Sometime tomorrow?" Old Drewes called.

"Nope. Gotta take care of it tonight. It's important."

"Welll . . . all right. Just a minute then."

Presently both old people emerged barefoot from their bedroom, Ma Pipp carrying the lamp. Ma Pipp had slipped on a pink kimono over her nightgown. She stood a good six inches taller than her man and about three times as broad and round. There was something about Ma Pipp that reminded Garrett of Laura more than a little. Old Drewes' white nightgown hung wrinkled to his banty calves. Beside his fat Belgian mare of a wife Old Drewes resembled a little Shetland stud.

Ma placed the lamp on the dining table, and the two old people sat down together on a horsehair sofa. Garrett and Laura took the loveseat across from them. The outline of a golden lion showed in the rich brown rug on the floor between them. Family photographs hung on the blue walls.

"Well, what is it?" Ma Pipp said. She was so thick she had a face that was completely round. Except for glinting black eyes there was no expression on it.

"Ya, son, what is it?" Old Drewes echoed. He was balding and had a heavy walrus mustache. His cheeks were sunken like the sections of a dried pumpkin.

"We might as well come right out flat with it," Garrett said. "Me and Laura are going to have a baby."

90

Ma Pipp sucked a big breath. "Eeeeth!" The sound of it was like the whistle of a pump with bad leathers.

Old Drewes' cheeks wrinkled up even more.

Laura began to bawl.

Garrett went on. "It's all my fault, too. Not Laura's."

"It's not either all his fault," Laura cried. "I'm just as guilty as he is."

Ma Pipp held herself big and tight together. "So you two want to get married now, hah?"

"That's the general idee," Garrett said. "Do we have your blessing?"

"Blessing, no. Permission, yes. Ha, Drewes?"

"Wal, ya, I guess so, But——"

"But, nothing." Ma Pipp gave herself a big shake. "Have you told your folks yet, Garrett?"

"We thought we'd tell you first."

"Hmm."

"I'll tell my folks when I get home tonight."

All of a sudden Old Drewes began to cry. His weeping was as loud as Laura's.

"What're you bawling about?" Ma Pipp roared, giving Old Drewes a punch in the ribs with her elbow, so hard he almost fell off the horsehair couch.

"The shame of it, oh, the shame of it," Old Drewes wept. "And my own daughter yet."

"Shame of it, nothing." Ma Pipp jerked Old

Drewes upright. "Shame? Hah! We weren't any better ourselves. We were just plain lucky I didn't get caught."

Garrett was considerably relieved by the favorable turn things had taken. And he had to fight back a smile. Good old Ma Pipp. Laura would be the same someday.

Meanwhile, Laura wept and wept.

Garrett went over and put his arms around Ma Pipp and gave the old lady a great big smack on her cheek, then went back to the loveseat and took Laura in his arms.

Ma Pipp lunged to her feet. "I'll make us all some hot chocalary. You like, Garrett?"

"You betcha I like chocalary."

5

Garrett and Laura sat waiting in their buggy outside the church. They were expecting to be called in at any moment and tell their story to the consistory. It was eight in the evening and getting dark. Garrett had unchecked Lady and she was grazing lustily in the grass between the parsonage and the church.

On the other side of the parsonage stood Big John's carriage and team of light-gray trotters. Mem Engleking had gone in to visit the reverend's wife. While Big John was attending the consistory meeting inside the church, young Alfred Engleking, whose job was to do nothing but drive for Big John, had slipped away to see Marie Memling.

Garrett gave Laura a warm smile. "You look much better now that you've thrown that corset away."

Laura cupped a hand over her belly. "But I look so lumpy. I know I sure feel lumpy."

"Don't talk like that. You don't know how much that lump becomes you. I'm glad to see it."

"They'll make us stand up in front of the whole church, won't they?"

Garrett held his blond head to one side. "Well, they can't very well make an exception for us. You know the church. What's good for one is good for all. We're all equal at the foot of God's throne."

"It's all over town too. That ought to be enough punishment."

"Girl, look, don't take it so hard. Remember, you must put your mind on what's good for the baby tomorrow, not on how you may feel today. Within a year it'll all be blown over. When they see the kid running around bright and happy, the people'll forget this black time."

"I hope so."

It was late June, and warm, and the darkening evening vibrated with cricket song. It was too warm to wear the yellow silk duster and Laura folded it neatly away.

A June bug came blundering out of the rose-

94

dusk sky in the west and whacked against Laura's cheek.

"Eeek!" Laura recoiled against Garrett. "Darn bugs," she said.

"Rather have them around than mosquitoes," Garrett said.

Laura leaned her head on his shoulder. "Mashing themselves all over my face."

"Cripes, it's hot with a suit jacket on." Garrett looked down at her for a second. "Sure wish it was over."

Laura sat very still for a moment; then jerked away. She sat as far away from Garrett as the buggy seat would allow. "Mister Garrett Engleking! I'm surprised at you."

Garrett threw back his white-gold pompadour with a quick lifting motion of his head. "Now what did I do?"

Laura regarded him steadily. There was love in her look but there was also disgust in it. "You know very well what I'm talking about."

"Now, wife——"

"I'm not your wife yet. And I won't be if you do it again."

"What are you talking about?"

"Garrett Engleking, you've been drinking."

"Only some homebrew."

"Smells stronger than homebrew to me."

95

"Alf has been making some again, getting it ready for threshing time. Like he always does. He and I sampled it to see if it was going to be all right."

"Garrett, will you tell me right here and now if that's all you had?"

Garrett's lower lip came out. It worked up and down several times, at last reached up and touched the tip of his nose. His white sun-scorched brows came together in a deep frown.

"Garrett?"

"Welll . . ."

"Or we can go home right now. I'll have this baby alone. By myself. I just simply won't have a drunkard for a husband."

The door to the church opened and Deacon Jacob Abt stood under the single front light. Deacon Abt looked around, then spotted them in their buggy. He crooked a finger at them, motioning them to come in.

Garrett acknowledged the crooked finger with a quick nod. He didn't much care for Jacob Abt. Abt was one of those busy fox-terrier kind of fellows you had to keep your eye on or he'd water all over your leg. Abt could be Christian-mean sometimes. How he'd been elected to the consistory had always been a puzzle to Garrett.

"We gotta get goin'," Garrett said.

96

Laura said, "You haven't answered my question yet."

"Oh, let's not have a fight just as we're about to confess our sin."

"We're going to have one if you don't answer me. I won't go in there until you answer me."

"Oh, all right." Garrett reached down to make sure Lady's reins were securely wrapped around the whip holder. "When I drove around the section to pick you up, I ran into the Hopkins boys. By their grove there."

"And?"

"You know how old man Hopkins is ag'in the world, making everything they need right there on the yard theirselves—oatmeal and cornmeal—how he won't buy anything out of a store exceptin' salt and sugar, even makin' his own raisins?"

"Yes?"

"Well, he and the boys make their own medicine now too."

"Medicine?"

"Medicine water. You know. Whiskey out of sour mash."

"So that's it! I knew it wasn't just homebrew beer on your breath. Too racy."

"You couldn't smell the difference."

"I could so. I could smell the Devil himself on your breath."

"Girl. Girl. I hope you're not going to be one of those——"

"——sourpuss crabs like my ma? I will be when it comes to alcohol. On other things, maybe no."

"It was just some of the Hopkins' own stuff."

"And one bottle of homebrew a day. I don't mind either. Taken just before supper. At the end of the day. But whiskey in any shape or form, no, no, no."

"All right, girl."

Laura smiled, and nodded once, quickly. "Now we're ready to go in."

Garrett couldn't help but smile a little himself. "What a gal you are."

"Shouldn't you tie Lady to a hitching post?"

"Her? Never."

"She won't run off?"

"If she does, it'll be our fault, not hers. She's smarter'n we are. You don't see her getting into any messes like we did."

"She let us get into trouble."

"She wasn't around that first time in the cornfield, remember?" Garrett helped Laura down the buggy step. "And she was safe in the barn eating hay that other time in the blizzard."

Laura smiled a private smile at Garrett. "She was with us all the rest of the other times though. Out in Sam Young's pasture."

"Ha! By then she knew it was already too late."

They mounted the church steps. June bugs swirled in erratic concentric circles around the single light over the front door. Another June bug whacked into Laura, this time on her primped-up dark hair.

Laura brushed it away. "Phew!"

The bug dropped to one of the wooden steps below. Laura promptly stepped down and squashed it under the heel of her button shoe.

Deacon Abt held the door open for them and they entered a small hallway. There was an instant smell of cigars and chewing tobacco. There was also a very faint aroma of peppermints about.

Deacon Abt glowered at them from under a throw of blond hair. It was plain to see he considered them the lowest of all congregational worms. He opened the consistory door next and ushered them inside. A single electric light burned in a smoke-filled room.

Much scraping of chairs followed, and both Reverend Tiller and the entire consistory turned to face the guilty pair. Deacon Abt sat Garrett and Laura at the near end of the table. Reverend Tiller sat at the head of the table. Six elders sat in a line down one side and six deacons on the other. Elder August Highmire, father of the four Highmire old maids, sat on the reverend's right, and Deacon Abt, ranking deacon, sat on the reverend's left. Elder Big John Engleking sat at the end of the line of elders, next to Garrett. The consistory was meant to be an exact reproduction of the Lord Jesus Christ and his twelve disciples. On the long pine table lay three books: a Bible, a church concordance, and a psalm book open at the form for the confession of fornication.

Thirteen pairs of consistory eyes sat in silence, examining the guilty couple hair for hair.

"Nuh," Reverend Tiller said from the head of the table. He put aside his cigar and folded his hands.

All eyes swung to the head of the table.

"We understand you two have something to announce that involves church discipline."

Garrett swallowed loudly. The sound of it was like the click of a hiccup. "Yes."

Reverend Tiller wiggled the tips of his folded fingers. The good reverend was a stocky man of some forty summers. He had a fine head of brown hair that had just begun to gray over the ears. His eyes were blue, his face round, his lips full and pink. He enjoyed being alive. Yet he had a duty to do and he had put on a formal air. "Is there anything in what you have to tell us that might stand in the way of your remaining a Christian Church man and woman?"

Garrett's throat pumped again. "There is."

"Can you tell us about it?"

"Well, you see, Reverend . . . Well, we're going to have a baby and we ain't married yet."

"In other words, you wish to confess fornication?"

"I guess. Yes."

"Nuh."

Garrett flushed a bluish red. Laura bit her lip.

"You freely admit to this?"

"Yes."

"You are both members of the church?"

"Yes."

"And you now wish to stand up in church and confess your sin before the assembled congregation? After the child is born, God willing?"

"Yes."

"And you do this having also in mind that you wish to have your child baptized into the church?"

"Yes."

"Do your parents know? Both of them?"

"Yes."

"You have your license to wed?"

"Yes."

"When do you plan to wed?"

"Next Saturday. If you will, Reverend."

"Nuh." Reverend Tiller looked from face to face around the pine table. "Is there anyone else here who wishes to ask the penitents a question?"

Deacon Abt cleared his throat. He lowered a

leonine look at Laura. "When do you expect the baby? Exactly."

Garrett looked sidelong at Laura.

Laura blinked, then looked Deacon Abt in the eye. "Late in September."

"I see."

Elder Highmire across the table next cleared his throat. Elder Highmire had a great head of hair too, shock white, with thick white brows. "How did this thing happen? Garrett, here, we already know about, what kind of a mess he can get into. He's got a weakness for them kind of things. He can't let it alone. But you, young lady, a nice Christian girl like you, how could you do a thing like that? Didn't you feel guilty doing it?"

"It just happened, is all," Laura said in a small voice.

"You didn't stop to think?"

"No. We was in love."

"Love, pah!"

"Well, we were."

"You know, of course, don't you, that it is only the married people who can do these things? That you're not supposed to be doing these things unless you intend to have children?"

"We did intend to have children."

"What? Before marriage?"

Laura looked down at her hands.

Eleven pairs of consistory eyes looked at Laura's swollen belly. Elder Engleking didn't look at Laura. He instead was looking at his folded hands. He sat very quietly inside his huge blue-clad bulk. His eyes, half-closed, were full of inward reverie. Reverend Tiller, meanwhile, was studying the ceiling in the dark above the lampshade.

Garrett volunteered, "It was really all my fault, not hers."

Elder Highmire's thick white brows rose as he swung his full attention on Garrett. "You forced yourself on her?"

Garrett swallowed. He was afraid the consistory could read in his eyes what he was hearing in his head. "Garrett," Laura had said, "be a devil for once."

Deacon Abt had further questions. "How did it happen? I mean, where were you? Out riding in your buggy?"

"Now, now," Reverend Tiller warned. "The questions need not be that particular, you know."

Deacon Abt said, "Reverend, I think we should know if it happened in a buggy. You yourself once preached on the evils of buggy riding out in the country for our young people."

"Yes, yes, I know." Reverend Tiller stared at the ceiling some more. "But in this case we don't need to be any further particular. These two covenant children have already freely confessed what many people never confess. And that is enough for now. If they had not it would be a different matter."

"I still think we should know if it happened in a buggy or not."

"And if it did?"

"Then you should preach another sermon on it. And we should make a ruling against letting our young folks ride around so free in the country."

Garrett broke in. "Well, if you really want to know, we did it in a bed. Between clean white sheets. In Sam Young's house."

Stiff silence.

Reverend Tiller's eyes came back to the table. "I think this has gone far enough." A mischievous look played at the corners of his eyes. He cleared his throat. "All this pick pick pick at these poor children. Remember, it is the lost sheep that is at last found that the Lord loves most."

Elder Highmire suddenly had red roses in his cheeks. "Yes, the ninety-and-nine who behave themselves, they're never given any credit for self-control and right living."

Reverend Tiller leaned back in his chair. "It reminds me of an experience I once had in my parish at Pella. Every Sunday there was this middle-aged couple sitting up front, almost under the pulpit. The woman was somewhat of a pusher. Ambitious. She had it in her heart that her husband should become a leading pillar in the church. She was always after him—be prompt this, be neat that. She always put on a good front for the Lord. Which was probably all right. Poor soul. But she was especially picky when it came to clothes. This one Sunday in particular I'm thinking about, I happened to catch her looking at her husband's collar. As I began to develop my sermon and entered into a discussion of my second point, I saw her secretly sneak over a hand and pick at a white thread sticking out of his shirt collar. She gave it a quick little jerk, like so, and snapped it off, and then, pretending she was paying extra close attention to me, she casually let the snip of thread fall to the floor under her bench. After a little while, her eyes ran over her husband's shirt collar again. Well, well. There was still some of that white thread sticking out. Again she secretly reached out a hand and gave the white thread a jerk, and after a bit let it fall to the floor. Pretty soon, looking yet again, she saw it was still there, a tiny piece of it. I tell you, all through that sermon she kept picking and picking at that endless snip of a thread. And all the while her poor husband sat quietly enduring it all. Never once did he blink his eyes. Well! the upshot of it all was that by the time I ended the sermon she had completely unraveled her husband's underwear off him out from under his blue suit. It all lay in a pile of white snips on the floor under her bench."

Laughter burst from every face around the pine table, including even Deacon Abt and Elder Highmire. And Garrett and Laura.

"So you see what happens if you look too close. And I don't think any of us here wants to pick pick pick at these fine honest young folk so that we finally unravel their underwear off them."

Deacon Abt raised a hand.

"Yes?"

"I have one final question though, Reverend, and then I'll let them go."

"Shoot."

Deacon Abt directed a bull's goring look at Garrett. "Brother Engleking, these awful things now, they just don't happen. It's true we're all born in sin, worms miserable in the sight of God, but yet, sometime, somewhere, the idea to do it has got to come from somebody. The Devil must have told you to do this, didn't he, ah?"

Garrett stared at Deacon Abt.

"Tell us, Brother Engleking, really, where did you learn about fornication? It was from the Devil, wasn't it? He whispered it into your ear."

Garrett turned white around the edges of his nostrils. He began to tremble. His mind flashed with all sorts of ideas. Then a certain thought came to him and he let fly. "I learned it from the Bible."

"The Bible?"

"Yes. Where it says in Genesis how Onan knew the seed would not be his, and it came to pass when he went in unto his brother's wife that he spilled it on the ground lest that he should give seed to his brother."

In the following silence fourteen watches ticked very loudly.

Garrett thought: "Now let just one of those pious bastards tell me I should've spilled it on the ground. Or on the white sheets."

Reverend Tiller harumphed. "Well, now, son, you know of course that the various events recorded in the Bible were not intended to be used as examples to live by so much as they are examples to be used for instruction. As warnings from God what not to do."

"Deacon Abt brought up the subject, Reverend. I didn't."

"Mmm."

"You know how it is: tell the truth and shame the Devil. If you must."

Laura flicked Garrett a look. She whispered under her hand, "Ask the deacon when his oldest daughter's birthday is. And then ask him the date when he got married."

Garrett nodded. He leaned with both elbows on the pine table. "Reverend?"

"Yes, my son."

"We came here of our own free will and told you what we done, didn't we?"

"Yes."

"When we could just as easy've gone away somewhere?"

"Yes."

"Or had the baby thrown? By that dirty old doctor over in Last Chance?"

"Yes."

"We just let it all fly out, didn't we? Freely confessed?"

"Yes."

"Reverend, since we wasn't at all sneaky about it, or small about it, why can't certain members of your consistory here be equally high-minded about it all?"

"Son, are you about to make an accusation?"

"Reverend, let's put it this way. Laura and I will accept the discipline of the church in this matter. Yes. Because we got it coming. We're big enough to be small enough for this one time. But are the members of this consistory big enough?"

"What do you mean, son?"

"Let me ask every one of you here this question." Garrett looked them all in the eye, one by one, up and down the table, thirteen of them. "Which one of you can honestly say you didn't do it with your wife before you got married?"

The bulb in the single lamp glimmered momentarily.

"Wasn't every single one of you just plain lucky you didn't get caught?" Garrett pointed the finger from face to face around the table. He wound up holding his finger in his father's face the longest. "In the old days, according to the Law of Moses, they used to stone people taken in adultery. What we should really do, Laura and me, is say unto you this: He that is without sin in this matter among you, let him be the first to cast a stone upon us. And this includes you too, Reverend."

Reverend Tiller relit his cigar and puffed a tremendous puff of smoke. As he did so his sharp blue eyes watched the confrontation between Big John the father and Garrett the son. Finally he said, "Nuh. Enough of this. What we want to know is this: Do you, Garrett Engleking, and do you, Laura Pipp, freely confess your sin in this matter up for our consideration?"

"We do. Not, Laura?"

Laura nodded.

"That is all we really need to know. You can go.

You will be told later what our decision is. Thank you. And goodnight."

Garrett and Laura pushed back their chairs and got to their feet.

Laura said steadily, "Thank you, Reverend. Thank you for your time."

"Not at all. Not at all."

About an hour later, Garrett and his father met again, in the dark out on the street. Garrett and Laura were heading for the north road out of Bonnie and Big John for the south road. Smart Ears Alfred, Garrett's younger brother, as usual sat in the driver's seat of his father's carriage. Big John and Mem rode regally in back.

"Hold up," Big John called.

Alfred drew the trotters up close. The carriage wheels stilled.

Garrett stopped on his side of the road.

Three vague white faces in the black carriage faced two vague white faces in the black buggy.

Mem spoke testily from her place. "Pa told me what you done in front of the minister. Have you no respect?"

"For you and Pa?"

"For the church, that's what."

"For the church, yes. So far. That's why we came at all."

"But not for us?"

"Do you deserve it?"

Mem swished her white fan across her long dark dress. She turned to her driver son. "Alfred, home! Right now, right away."

"Wait," Big John grumped from his big belly. He held up his hand. An Old Country ring on his finger sparkled in the starlight. "Garrett, ain't you wondering what the consistory decided?"

"Sure I'm wondering. But I'll be darned if I ask you. I'll wait until the minister tells me."

Mem said, "Alfred, drive home. I see that one of your father's sons wants to be stubborn in his sin."

Laura threw Mem a glittering, almost venomous look across the buggy wheels.

Big John chewed on one of the tufts of his heavy mustache. "Well, I might as well tell you. Reverend asked me to. The consistory decided to accept your confession."

"Good. Not, Laura?"

"Yes. Good." Laura snuggled closer to Garrett.

"You're to stand up and confess it before the congregation when it comes time to baptize the baby."

"All right."

"And if the baby should not live at birth, you're to confess anyway."

"Whatever the Lord gives."

"Scandalous!" Mem hissed. "And my own son yet."

"Be honest now, Mem. Isn't it true that you and Pa were just plain lucky?"

"Alfred, drive home! One of my own sons has become too proud to be humble in his sin. Repentant."

Garrett couldn't help but smile a bit devilishly. "Mem, we'll be over for coffee after church when the baby is finally baptized."

"Hnrff."

Big John asked, "Where will you two live?"

Garrett could sense from the sound of the old man's voice that Big John was also smiling to himself a little. "We've rented the lower floor of that redstone house on the corner. Opposite the Congregational Church."

"Alf got himself a new hired hand yet?"

"Alf thinks he can make it alone for the rest of the year with his oldest boy Free. Except for maybe corn picking."

"How'll you make a living?"

"I'm opening my store again."

"With what?"

"Laura's pa settled some money on us."

"Hmm." Big John folded his hands over his belly. "Well, all I can say then is: Son, this time give no credit. Not even to anybody from our church. You've got to be tougher."

"Thanks."

"Goodnight."

" 'Night."

"At last!" Mem cried.

6

Laura's baby was born dead.

Garrett asked the doctor how come.

Dr. Fairlamb scowled. His black hair came up in a ridge as firm as the bristles of a new hairbrush.

The three of them were sitting in Dr. Fairlamb's office where Garrett had taken Laura for a final checkup.

Dr. Fairlamb said, "There's no accounting for it. It just happens. In the best of families."

"Maybe if we'd've done something different . . ."

"No, no. In fact, you're probably lucky it was born dead."

"How so?"

"It would have probably been a bad baby had it lived. Malformed."

"I see."

"Let's just say that the good Lord never really meant for it to be born."

"I see."

"Now don't worry about it, you two. Try again." Dr. Fairlamb pulled at a heavy Waldemar chain hanging across his vest and took out his watch. "Well, I've got to be going."

Laura was as pale as a sunburned turnip. "Was it alive long enough to have a soul, doctor?"

"How should I know? Certainly not on this side of the womb."

"I mean, in me."

"It had to be alive at first."

"I mean, until how late was it alive?"

"It was probably alive until a couple of weeks ago."

"Ahh," Laura said. "Then we better bury it in that plot we bought, Garrett."

"All right," Garrett said.

"Well, you two, better luck next time," Dr. Fairlamb said.

"Thanks."

Garrett thought: "Another of my seed born dead. And this one blue." Garrett cried inwardly.

"My darling June Memling, she died of the green gangrene." Then Garrett thought: "But at least this time we saved the mother."

Out in their buggy again, Garrett put his arms around Laura and hugged her.

Laura suffered him. "I suppose we still got to stand up in church."

"I'm afraid so."

"We'll do it. We did it and we'll do it."

The confession before all the congregation went off smoothly. The church was full for once, which made Garrett grumble some, but nobody pointed the finger at them with their eyes. Most of the congregation felt sorry for them. Especially for Garrett.

Garrett and Laura were the last to step out of the side door into the bright sunlight. For a few seconds the people stood apart from them. Then tall Ada Alfredson moved out of the crowd and came up and said, "I hope nobody's asked you over for coffee yet."

Laura pulled down her corset. Laura had of late put on weight. "No, nobody has."

"Good. Then you two can stop by."

Garrett gave Ada a grudging smile. "Thanks, Ade, old girl. If worst comes to worst you're still always a friend, I see."

Ada smiled gravely. "If the Lord can forgive, I surely can."

7

In the last baseball game of the year, Bonnie beat
Hello, 11-7, and the Bonnie boys in celebration each
had a couple bottles of homebrew beer. The Engleking homebrew was known to have quite a wallop
and the boys showed it. Especially Garrett. Garrett
had caught a good game, had hit a tremendous home
run that cleared the cottonwoods along the back of
Ten Besten's grove, and had coaxed a pretty well-
pitched performance out of their young lefthander,
Walt Memling.

Garrett dropped off his two younger brothers

Albert and Robert at the Engleking place, then headed into town for a cup of Laura's chocalary.

It was still light out. The sun had just set. Riding specks of dust glimmered a faint gold in the still air. Flushed with a great victory and copious drafts of farm beer, and still wearing his gray baseball suit, Garrett sang himself a lonely ditty. His baritone voice carried a long way in the fall twilight. He sang to the rhythmic clopping of Lady's hooves on the hard dirt road. "Oh, I wish I had the wings of an angel, over these prison walls I would fly."

Lady seemed to relish the singing. Her long arched chestnut neck swayed swanlike from side to side.

Then up ahead Garrett saw another buggy coming toward them. Peering, he made out Bachelor Bill Tamming and his big red nose. Bachelor Bill was coming home from town.

Garrett cursed under his breath. "The dumb bustard is in my lane."

The best track was on the north or Garrett's side of the road. Bachelor Bill's side was soft and slow-going.

Bachelor Bill was driving a high-striding black gelding called Star. He had just put the whip to Star and the black gelding came on with flying out-thrown hooves. Star had a big white spot between the eyes. Coming at Garrett from the west, and directly in Garrett's track, Star looked exactly like a one-eyed monster.

"Hey, you!" Garrett called in warning.

Bachelor Bill stood up in his buggy, silk duster falling to his feet. "Better get out of my way, you baseball player!" he roared. "Or my horse will run you down."

Garrett sat up slowly. The pleasant aromas of victory and homebrew vanished from his brain. "The dirty bustard. The great big bully. Thinking he owns this two-mile stretch between his place and town. We'll see about that, we will. Hee-up, Lady. We're not afraid of him."

Lady had already pretty much decided on her own counsel. Her ears were shot straight ahead and she appeared to have risen a little in her flowing gait. She set herself for the collision.

"Get out of my way, you lazy baseball player! Pull over! Make way for the bigger horse! Or he'll run you into the ditch!"

Garrett braced himself too. He smiled the old arrogant Engleking smile. "I'm game if you are. Let's just see once who'll be the first to pull over."

On the horses rushed, heads high, ears working, knees glancing shiny in the dusty gold light, nostrils spraying phlegm.

At the last second Lady put on an extra burst of speed.

121

"Pull over!" Bachelor Bill bellowed.

Garrett smiled.

The horses hit. Buggies upended, rear wheels spinning high. There was a high-pitched scream from one of the horses.

Bachelor Bill was catapulted up and out of his buggy. His long heavy body made two complete somersaults in midair, and he landed with a whumpfing whack flat on his back on the hard-packed side of the road.

Garrett found himself spilling headfirst into the ditch. His nose dug a furrow through the curly buffalo grass.

Again one of the horses screamed.

Garrett was the first to get to his feet. He'd recognized the scream. It was Lady.

Garrett tore into the tangled mass of ripped harnesses and broken shafts and bent buggy wheels. Both horses were lying flat on their sides, Lady one way, Star the other way. Lady was bleeding something fierce from her broad chest while Star was only knocked out. The left point of Star's shafts had gone into Lady a full foot deep. Lady's blood bubbled a sheening purple in the gold twilight.

"Holy Habakkuk! Now I've gone and done it," Garrett said.

A groan rose from Bachelor Bill. He lay on the ground behind them.

"I should've known he'd be a bullhead to the end."

Another groan rose from Star underfoot.

"Too bad my Lady's shafts couldn't've rammed Bill's old plug instead. The other way around. She was more worth saving than his old hayburner."

The wheels on the upper side of both buggies were still spinning. The spokes gave off a silvery whizzing reflection.

Squatting, Garrett tried to extract the shaft point from Lady's chest.

Lady stirred. She reared her head a little with a strange jerky undulation. She opened her mouth and blood rose with a rush from it like water from a cistern pump. Red splashed all over Garrett's gray baseball suit. Lady groaned deep in her belly. After a moment the groan emerged as a wet mutter from the ragged hole in her chest. Then Lady slumped.

Garrett went around to where Bachelor Bill lay. "Get up, you great big overgrown camel you." He gave Bachelor Bill a tremendous kick in the ass. "I hope to God you broke your great big hump of a nose. It'd serve you right if you did, killing my Lady." Garrett gave Bachelor Bill another kick in the butt. "Get up."

Bachelor Bill's eyes slowly opened. "Where am I?"

"In hell, if you want to know. Get up on those

123

clodhopper feet of yours." Garrett aimed another powerful kick at Bachelor Bill. "Up!"

Bachelor Bill stumbled up. "What happened?"

"C'mere!" Garrett grabbed Bachelor Bill by the neck and steered him toward the tangled mass of horseflesh and buggy wheels. "See that! Well, you dumb bustard, you just got through killing one of the finest pacers God ever made. Look at her. You can at least help me pull your damned shaft out of her lungs."

Garrett forced Bachelor Bill to kneel beside him. And finally, grunting, wallowing in purplish blood, they extracted the shaft point. To their surprise, Lady raised her head yet once more, fluttered her nostrils at them, and died.

Tears ran down Garrett Engleking's face.

Bachelor Bill was so rattled he offered to pay for everything: for Lady, the broken buggy, the harness. Right then and there.

Garrett took him up on it. "Have you got the cash with you? It'll cost you exactly five hundred bucks."

"That much?"

"Wait'll we tell the sheriff what side of the road you was on."

"I got some money hidden in the milk shed. Come."

"And you can clean up the mess too. Call the rendering works."

"Ain't you gonna bury your own horse?"

"What for? She's yours now."

Star came to, and they helped the big black gelding to its feet.

At Bachelor Bill's house, Bachelor Bill offered to give Garrett a ride home to Bonnie.

Garrett stuck the fat wad of greenbacks into the back pocket of his baseball pants. "No, thanks."

Catcher's mitt and his home run bat under an arm, Garrett started off in the dark.

8

In the next couple of months Garrett and Laura
became as ardent a pair of lovers as God ever made.
Laura had put on a little weight but Garrett didn't
mind. He had given up his notion that a slim wife
was the thing for him. He made smiling jokes about
Laura being nice and warm to sleep against in the
winter. "She may be as big as a stove, yes, but she
sure is softer. And if you're real careful you can
sometimes even kiss her without getting burned."

But make love as they might they had no luck.
Her periods came as regular as a clock every quarter
moon. She wasn't off by as much as a day.

Two years went by. Still no children.

At last they went to Dr. Fairlamb to ask him about it.

Old Doc gave Laura a thorough examination. He told them Laura was perfectly all right; said for them just to keep trying. "And you might try playing at it. Fool around a little more. Don't be quite so serious about it. Relax."

"We're just having a little hard luck then?"

"That's it. That's it. And you might try different positions."

"Like having her play the papa?"

"That's it."

Another year went by. Still no luck.

When a fourth year went by and still no baby, Garrett suggested they adopt a child.

Laura was game.

"Good," Garrett said. "I've just simply got to have some kids around. I was raised in a big family where there was always some kids underfoot. And I surely miss that."

"Same with me."

Garrett thought: "Yes, maybe I could've lived with June Memling without kids in her case. But not with Laura. Though Laura sure is a good one. A real sport. Not one of those goddam complainers."

About that time Garrett began to drink a little, spiking his beer with Excelsior alcohol. Laura, to keep him company, and to keep him somewhat in line, drank with him.

A salesman from Sioux City came by one day and told in Garrett's shop about "them two little orphan boys who'd lost their pa and ma in that Floyd River flood."

Garrett perked up. "How old are they?"

The salesman set down his leather case. He was a dark, dapper fellow about thirty years old. "The biggest is around two. But the little one is only a month old."

Garrett chewed his nether lip.

Clean hardware—hammers, guns, saws, brace-and-bits, forks, shovels—gleamed in neat rows all around them in the store. Sweet sawdust lay yellow down the main aisle.

"They're having trouble finding a home for them," the salesman went on to say.

"You know the address?"

"It's in the morning paper, I think."

When Garrett went home at noon, he announced he'd closed up shop and they were taking a trip in their car to Sioux City. Garrett had bought a Chevie sedan with the money he'd got for Lady and his buggy.

Laura sat stubborn for a minute. "What for?" The last time they had gone to Sioux City Garrett had spent part of the time trying to locate an illegal case of Excelsior alcohol.

"Get your glad rags on. T'ain't what you think."

"Promise, Garrett?"

"Promise."

They found the two orphans in a little town called Hinton just outside Sioux City. A minister and his wife were caring for them until a home could be found for them. When the minister discovered what church Garrett and Laura belonged to, he was more than enthusiastic about them becoming the foster parents of the orphans. He began to praise the little tykes to the skies.

The truth was they were fine little kids. As sweet as harvest apples. The older one, Harvey, had hair like Garrett himself, white-gold. It was as if he might have been one of Garrett's own. The baby, still unnamed, already had a little silver forelock.

Garrett fell in love with them on the spot. So did Laura. While Garrett playfully bounced Harvey on his knee, Laura sat squeezing the baby in her arms with tender mother hugs.

Later, as they were leaving, Garrett told the minister, "Now don't you let anybody else have them. Because you'll be hearing from us."

Out in the Chevie, as they purred home to Bonnie, Laura said, "Garrett, I'll be glad to be their ma. Only there's one thing."

"What?"

"No more spiked beer."

"Well I'll be cowkicked. That's just what I was thinking. All right, Ma. For them kids, anything."

They applied to the church consistory for permission to adopt the children.

It was again a softly quiet night in June. Jacob Abt was still head deacon, August Highmire was still head elder, and Reverend Tiller as usual sat at the head of the table. Cigar smoke drifted up in lazy spirals into the immediate radiance of the single light.

"Nuh." Reverend Tiller put aside his cigar. "Nuh. Mr. and Mrs. Engleking, we understand that you two have something to announce that involves church matters?"

"We do," Garrett said.

Twelve sets of eyes, including those of Elder Big John Engleking, stared at Garrett and Laura with lifted, wondering looks. What had this restless Garrett Engleking got himself into now?

"Reverend, as you know, the Lord has not yet blessed us with children. And we're lonesome for some kids. We'd like to have a houseful of them."

"God's will."

"Yes. But it begins to look as if it is His will that we ain't supposed to have any of our own blood. So, we been thinking . . . we been thinking of adopting some."

131

"Nuh. Well. Yah."

"Truth is, Laura and me here, we've found us a couple of kids we'd like to adopt."

"Nuh?"

Laura dug a couple of photographs out of her purse.

Reverend Tiller held up his hand. "Uk—uk—before we look at them, let us have you answer a few questions first."

"Shoot, Reverend."

"They are orphans, you say?"

"Yep. Their pa and ma drowned in that Floyd River flood."

"In what denomination were these children baptized?"

"We don't know. The minister in whose house we saw them said he didn't know either."

"So." Reverend Tiller picked up his cigar.

"From what he said, I don't think the parents went to church much."

Deacon Abt stuck in a horn. "Are the children baptized at all?"

"We don't care if they ain't. We'll start 'em fresh in our church here. We'll baptize 'em right here in Bonnie."

Elder Highmire broke in. "Now wait a minute. Our church can't just accept any old kid that comes along. We have to know if they was born covenant children or not. Born to a covenant family."

"What difference does that make when we can start 'em off brand-new in the Christian Church?" Garrett protested. "They'll never know the difference."

Laura put in, "They're just babies, both of them. So far as they'll ever know, we'll be the only parents they'll ever have. They'll just be like one of us."

"Any old kid," Garrett snorted. He crossed his white brows at Elder Highmire. "How do you know but what you wasn't born an orphan and you was never told?"

"If I was born an orphan," Elder Highmire shouted, "you can be doggone sure that my parents knew I was born a covenant child or not somewhere." Elder Highmire was suddenly so mad his mop of white hair worked up into a regular Indian war bump.

"Now, now," Reverend Tiller warned.

Deacon Abt had to horn in some more. "If you can't show us that those two orphan kids you want to adopt ain't full pedigreed covenant children, we can't have them. They're of the Devil."

Laura had a black look for the good deacon. "Those two cute kids, who don't know no better, they are of the Devil?"

"Yes sir! And you know what the Lord did with

the Devil when the Devil was still an angel. The Lord threw the Devil into hell. Where there shall be much wailing and gnashing of teeth." Deacon Abt was so fanatically worked up he beat the tabletop with a small, hard fist. Boom. Boom. "That's what I say."

Garrett was astounded. "Are you trying to tell me that the Lord's already thrown these two poor little innocent tykes into hell? That they'll never have no chance at salvation?"

"I'm trying to tell you that for us to let you two adopt those two orphan kids," Deacon Abt said, "we've got to know if they was born a covenant child or not. That is, that they was born in a church which is . . . ah . . . ah . . ."

"Recognized," Reverend Tiller supplied.

"Yes, recognized. That is, recognized by our Christian Church. That's it."

Reverend Tiller held up the palms of both hands. "Nuh. Just a moment now. Everybody. Let's all sit back a minute and have a smoke together. Light up and think a minute. Let our nerves settle down a little." Reverend Tiller smiled at Laura. "As for you, Mrs. Engleking, we don't expect you to light up a pipe, but . . . ha ha . . . perhaps you have a peppermint with you?"

Laura blinked, and smiled back.

When all had lighted up, and Laura had slipped

a little white candy in her mouth, Reverend Tiller tipped back in his chair and began telling them another of his apt stories.

"It was when I had the charge at Squaw Tit, South Dakota." Reverend Tiller threw a quick twinkling look around the table. "We tried very hard to get the name of that town changed, by the way, but there were some old-timers down at the pool hall who liked the town's name just the way it was, and since they had an in with the city hall gang, we just couldn't make any headway." Reverend Tiller's lips worked as if he might be repressing a smile. "We had in that church there a young boy of around thirteen who was quite hard to handle. He was always into some kind of mischief. Making rattling noises on windows just when old maids were going to bed at night. Putting thumb tacks on my pulpit seat. Ha. Filling the wine jug for Lord's Supper with vinegar colored with red ink. Letting go a couple of bats right in the middle of my sermon. Oh, he was a regular rascal all right and his name was Billy." Reverend Tiller cleared his throat. "One day I decided I had a good job for Billy. I elected him organ pumper. That way I'd have him right under my nose while I preached. He needed the money too. He was an only son of a widow. Well, he seemed to like the job and things went along fine for a while.

He behaved himself. Every time the organist got up to play, he got up to pump."

Reverend Tiller blew up a little twisting tornado of a puff. "Well, one Sunday it was time again for my sermon on why it was, how it was, that God cast Satan into hell." The reverend allowed his musing eyes to rest on Deacon Abt a moment. "Or, as our esteemed deacon here puts it, when 'the Lord threw the Devil into hell.' Yes. Well, I had got pretty well along into my sermon, when I noticed two things going on right below my nose at the same time. One, that Elder Overacker, sitting on the aisle, had gone sound to sleep with his head thrown back and his mouth wide open. Two, that Billy, right across the aisle from Elder Overacker, was busy looking at Overacker's big open mouth with a very curious expression in his eyes—that Billy was very carefully biting on a gum wrapper and wadding it up into a little ball. Well! right away I knew we were in for another one of Billy's stunts. He was going to throw that wadded up gum wrapper into the good elder's open mouth. Yet, what could I do? I was preaching the Lord's word, the Lord was speaking through me, and I couldn't very well break in on these solemn thoughts and take the time to bawl Billy out. Or, for that matter, I couldn't very well stop right in the middle of my sermon and wake up old man Overacker either. The only thing I could think of doing was to raise my voice, to roar if need be, even if that particular part of the sermon didn't call for it. So I began to stomp and to roar. I railed from one side of the pulpit, pointing the finger this way and that, almost, yes, almost sticking my finger right into the old elder's mouth. Didn't do any good. Elder Overacker snored on. Then I railed from the other side of the pulpit, pointing the finger, pointing as it were at hell itself, as though the blazing snapping flames were right there at my very feet, verily. I shook my fist this way and that, almost, yes, almost right onto the chewing jaw of that rascal Billy's face. Didn't do any good. Not a particular. As far as those two were concerned—Elder Overacker and Billy the rascal—I might as well have been practice-preaching in front of my mirror at the parsonage. Though I should tell you, of course, that the rest of the congregation was enjoying it all. I was a-giving them one of my better sermons. I could just see some of the old gray sages getting ready with their compliments for after the church service."

Reverend Tiller's cigar had gone out and he relit it. "Well, now. All kinds of things were going through my head. That somehow better sense would take over in Billy's conscience itself—of which there wasn't much. Or that Elder Overacker would wake up. Or that the elder next to Overacker would give him a jab in the ribs. Or, as a last resort, that I simply

137

end the sermon right then and there even though I knew that God still had an awful lot to say for that day." Reverend Tiller flashed another quick twinkling look around at all fourteen assembled faces. "Well, what I actually did was to quick get to the climax of the sermon. Pronto. I told how the Lord God Jehovah was finally faced with the awful problem of having to throw Satan, throw the Devil, into the everlasting fires of hell itself. Much as He hated to do this, because after all Satan had always been his favorite angel, and his leading angel. He simply had to do it. Yes, finally, at last, yes, God decided to throw the source of all evil into hell. Just then, Billy took the wadded up gum wrapper out of his mouth, and made a practice motion to throw it, and then did throw it, and I saw the little ball go arching across the aisle, and then, well, I just couldn't help myself, but I hit that pulpit a mighty whack, and I cried out, 'Verily! He threw 'em in there!' "

After that one even Elder Highmire slapped his leg in laughter.

Talk was once more pleasant for a while.

Yet Elder Engleking had a question or two. "Uh, son, how are things going now at the hardware store?"

"Fine."

"Are you still giving credit?"

Laura spoke up. "He's doing much better at it,

Pa. I'm there a lot and I make sure that the poor payers pay cash."

"That's fine, my girl. But will you have time to tend store when the children come?"

"Well, no, I guess maybe not."

Garrett worked his white brows at his father. "What's that got to do with it?"

Big John hauled his bulk upright in his chair. He returned an equally crisp white-browed look. "Just that we must make sure them children will be well-provided for, son."

"Holy Habakkuk! What difference does it make if I do give out a little credit now and then to some of those poor devils. So long as I pay my own debts?"

"You could be better off. And you wouldn't be so apt to go broke again like that first time. Bankrupt."

Reverend Tiller interposed. "Well now, perhaps, Brother Engleking, I mean the younger Brother Engleking, perhaps we should examine this strange custom of yours. What is it, why can't you ask people to pay cash?"

Garrett said stoutly, "I don't like to push people around. I don't like to embarrass people asking 'em head-on for money when I know they'll get around to paying up someday. They will if they can. It seems to be the Christian way to me."

"Hmm."

One of the elders halfway down the table, Old John Cooper, had a different question to ask. "Uh, Brother Engleking, it has often been rumored around town that . . . uh . . . like some of the other Englekings"—Elder Cooper threw a sly look at Elder Big John Engleking—"you like the drink pretty well. What do you have to say to that?"

Too quickly, Laura said, "Oh, Garrett's already promised there'll be no more Excelsior alcohol around if we get the kids."

"Excelsior?" Elder Cooper exclaimed.

"If you get the kids?" Deacon Abt cried.

"Now, now," Elder Highmire said, "if that's the way it is, why then I'm afraid I'm surely going to take a pretty sour look at the idea of you two adopting them kids. At all."

Garrett addressed the head of the table. "Reverend?"

"Yes, son."

"Doesn't it say in the Bible, in Luke there I think, 'Suffer the little children to come unto me, and forbid them not, for of such is the kingdom of God'? You remember that was when some people brought Jesus some little infants, that he would touch them, when his disciples rebuked them for doing it?"

"True."

"Well, then, ain't that what Laura and me are

doing, bringing them to you, and these here disciples are rebuking us for doing it?"

"Hmm."

Deacon Abt wasn't apt to let go once he had his teeth sunk into a problem. "Garrett, you've raised pigs, ain't you?"

"Some."

"And you know that to have a good litter of pigs, a good run of them, you need good breeding stock?"

"Sure."

"The sow needs to be of good stock?"

"Sure."

"But most of all you need a good sire, a first-class boar?"

"Sure."

"Better yet, if you got a boar with good pedigree papers, you'll get an even better litter of pigs?"

"Sure."

"Well, that's the way it is here with us Christian Churchers. We've got to know where everybody comes from. Someday those two boys will be fathers in their turn. And if they're in our church, we won't be able to say for sure that we've got good covenant papers for them."

Garrett came back with his own likening. "Abt, can I ask you a question?"

"Fire away."

"You've raised pigs too?"

"Some."

"And you've had it already where one sow had only three pigs survived and another sow had eleven?"

"Hmm."

"And you took four from the one who had eleven and put 'em in with the sow that had but three?"

"I guess so."

"Did those four pigs you put with the first sow, did they suffer?"

"I can't say they did."

"Did either sow ever suffer by it?"

"I guess no."

"That's what Laura and me want to do here. Except that it's even worse. These two poor little pigs lost their mother."

Cigars glowed.

But the vote went unanimous against Garrett and Laura anyway.

9

Garrett went into a tight-lipped rage. And he decided to do something about it. He found out that the Big Christian Church across town didn't have such strict rules about accepting orphans into the church, so he promptly withdrew his and Laura's church papers from the Little Christian Church and joined the Big Christian Church, and then went out and adopted the two blond little orphans from Hinton, and had them baptized.

For several months Bonnie was in an uproar over this maneuver. Not one of the Englekings dropped by for coffee after church at Garrett and

Laura's. Not one of the church members came in to do business with him at the store. Of course in the meantime Garrett and Laura had a lot of sudden new coffee-klatch friends from the worldly set in town. And Garrett also had a lot of new business at the store from the Big Christian Church membership, more than ever in fact.

Two years went by.

During that time there was a change of ministers in the Big Christian Church. And an election in the Little Christian Church swept out most of the members of the old consistory, among them Deacon Abt, Elder Highmire, Elder Cooper and Elder Engleking.

Then Garrett made his next move. He used the excuse that he couldn't stand the new Big Christian Church minister and asked to have his church papers back. When he got them, he promptly asked the new consistory in the Little Christian Church if he and his wife couldn't come back.

It worked. He was welcomed back to his old church—with his two adopted boys as baptismal members.

One thing, however, didn't work. He and Laura still had no issue of their own blood.

10

Free was through college and was back in Bonnie to pick up some odd jobs to tide him over until fall.

One week Free got a job at Sherm Engleking's place. Sherm was Free's uncle, Ada's younger brother, and only three years older than Free. Sherm and Garrett were on the same softball team together, the Homebrews at Hello, and on a couple of occasions Free had played with them.

It was June. Chickens were taking long trips into the alfalfa field. Yellow mustard under the blue sky was a waving green delight. Old sows in the mud beside the watertank resembled great rubber blisters.

The leathers in the mill pump below the hog-house needed replacing and Sherm phoned Garrett to fix them. Garrett had given up the hardware store again and was now doing nothing but straight plumbing work.

Free had heard an occasional whiff of gossip about Garrett—that Garrett still gave out too much credit and that he drank steadily a little. Free had himself seen Garrett take a nip before a ball game and later had smelled a kind of fermented pickle-juice on him.

When Sherm finished phoning, he told Free there seemed to be something the matter with Garrett's pickup. Would Free take the Ford and drive into town and help Garrett get it started? Maybe give him a push? Or at worst just bring Garrett and his wrenches out?

Sherm stood very slim in patched overalls. He had the Engleking sunburned white brows and when he frowned he also had the true Engleking look. "Something don't sound right at Garrett's this morn-ing. So take it easy when you poke your head into the door."

"Okay."

"Better get Allie here some groceries too while you're at it." Sherm gave his tall dark-haired wife a warm clap on the seat. "Huh, Al?"

Allie smiled like a lily. She was a Pipp, a younger

sister of Laura, and where Laura was chunky Allie was slender. Allie said, "I need a packet of needles. From Rexroth's there."

"Write it down," Free said.

Allie did.

Taking the slip of paper, Free folded his lanky frame in under the Ford steering wheel and drove off for town.

Free got the packet of needles first; also some Velvet tobacco for his pipe; then headed for Garrett's home.

He knocked on the kitchen door.

No answer.

"Garrett?" Free called. "I'm ready to take you out to Sherm's."

No answer.

Free next politely pushed open the door and looked inside.

Nobody in the kitchen. But the kettle was boiling. Yes, something wasn't right at Garrett's.

Free stepped with circumspect delicacy into the living room.

There sat Laura in a big blue easy chair with her two adopted boys, Harvey and Chester, in her lap. She had her arms around them, so tight it was as if she were afraid someone were going to snatch them from her. Her eyes were bloodshot and tears were running red streaks down her cheeks. A fore-

147

noon sun struck through the bay window, hitting the blue rug at her feet a glancing blow, and then casting a blue pallor over her arms and face.

"Laura?"

Laura didn't move. She only sat crying. The two towheads in her lap looked at her and then looked at Free. Their blue eyes studied Free from shadowed infant recesses. They almost had the look of collie puppies found with their mother hurt.

Free took a deep breath, and asked, "What's going on around here?"

Tears.

"Where's Garrett?"

A long deep sigh lifted up both her and the two boys.

"Harvey, where's your pa?"

Harvey gave Free the eyes of a stunned bunny.

"Chester?"

Chester looked from Free to Harvey to his mother. Said nothing.

A tinkling sound came from below.

Free pricked an ear. Garrett? That had to be Garrett. Garrett was somewhere in the basement. Free turned and headed for the stairway door. He hit the bottom step just as he spotted Garrett in the gloom.

Garrett was trembling, shivering even, as he hovered over a worktable. His blue shirt was tat-

148

tered, his overalls spotted, his shoes shapeless. On the table were lined up several rows of flashing hip-pocket pints. It was one of the pint bottles that had made the tinkling sound.

"Hey, what goes on here?" Free asked in a sudden voice.

Garrett turned slowly. His hands shook like the fingers of a pair of empty gloves in the wind. "Hi, Free."

"What in the world are you doing here? Sherm's been waiting all morning for you, man."

"Can't find the gas to get going." Garrett's face had the color of bled flesh and his eyes were like two big drops of curdled milk.

"You mean gas for your pickup?"

"Well . . . yeh . . . that too."

"What do you mean?"

Garrett gave Free a tormented look. It was the look of a dog who once might have run him off the property but now had to accept him with its tail between its legs.

"God, Garrett, I hate to be nosy, but Sherm told me to come and get you and all, so . . . What's the matter, old buddy?"

Garrett quickly grabbed hold of the edge of the worktable to keep from falling down.

"Garrett?"

"Well, boy, it's this way. If I don't get that shot in the morning I can't move around much."

"You mean alcohol?"

Garrett's eyes rolled; came to rest on the rows of pint bottles.

Free stepped closer. He picked up one of the pints. All the pints had the Excelsior label on them and all were empty. "You really don't need it that bad, do you?"

"Boy, if I don't get that shot right now I'm gonna die of the galloping shivers."

"What about those two little boys of yours upstairs?"

"Can't be helped." A frown chased across Garrett's blond brows. "And while you're at it why don't you ask about them other two boys? You know, them other'n I never had? Hah?"

"Garrett, really, if you need the drink that bad, man, why don't you go get yourself a pint and drink up?"

"I've run plumb out of money. My bootlegger won't let me have any more on credit. And Laura won't let me pawn any more of our furniture."

Free remembered the great home runs Garrett had hit for Bonnie in his day. Free wept dry-eyed.

"Yep, it's tough titty, boy. Didn't have any groceries in the house either this morning. Not even coffee. Rexroth won't give us any more on credit."

150

"You're still working."

"I know. I know. But collections 've been poor lately."

"You still can't be tough enough to get what's coming to you."

"Ain't got the heart to, boy."

Free remembered the wonderful leather mittens Garrett had once bought him.

"Do me a favor, will you, boy? For old time's sake?"

"If it'll help you get going, sure."

"Take these pints here and see if there ain't just one little drop left in them. Pour all the drops into one bottle and maybe there'll be enough for one swallow."

Free shook his head. "Garrett, I'm sorry, but that's against my principles."

"It's ag'in my religion too, boy, but yet I need it to get going to Sherm's. Today. Now. Sherm will pay me without my asking and then I can get the wife and kids some grub."

"And yourself another pint."

"You betcha. Be a good sport."

"I can't."

"Well, boy, I can't do it either." Garrett picked up one of the pints and tried to hold its mouth over the mouth of another pint. But his hands shook so much that he not only missed but was in danger of chipping the bottles. "See?"

Free's eyes clouded over. Poor Garrett. Poor poor devil. Then Free silently took the pint from Garrett and did it for him. Working patiently, holding the one over the other, Free managed to coax several drops out of each pint. When they were all added up, out of some sixty bottles, he had a half-jigger of pure Excelsior alcohol.

"Ah," Garrett cried, and he seized the pint the alcohol was in and threw it down the hatch in one swift gulp. "Now for a chaser of water from the tap." And again Garrett drank up. Garrett next got out his pipe and Prince Albert and lit up with a flourish. The transformation in him was miraculous. Color returned to his cheeks, his hand steadied, and the curdles of skim milk in his eyes became a solid blue.

Free stared and inwardly cried some more to himself. This great man this low.

Garrett rubbed his hands. "Now if we can just siphon a little gas out of Sherm's Ford into my pickup we can be on our way."

"Your pickup's otherwise okay then?"

"You betcha. Let's go."

Garrett did fine work that day. He pulled up the rods in Sherm's well and replaced the leathers. He found a crack in the sandpoint and welded it shut. He climbed the tower and greased the mill itself.

And finally he installed a little invention of his own so Sherm could shut down the mill from the house by pulling up on a wire tied to a wooden lever.

That night they all drove over to Hello for a softball game—Garrett and family, Sherm and wife, and Free. All three men played great ball, especially Garrett. Garrett hit three home runs. Laura and the boys and Allie cheered him on. So far as Free knew all Garrett had to drink was that half-shot collected for him in the morning out of all those empty pints. There was only a vague fermented pickle smell about him all that day.

On the way home, all riding in Garrett's Chevie, Garrett driving, with Allie and Sherm in the front seat, and Free and Laura and the boys in back, Garrett surprised them all by pulling a bottle out from under his seat.

"Where'd you get that?" Sherm demanded.

Garrett waggled his head. "I bet one of our boys I'd hit three home runs tonight. And I did it."

"I don't like that," Sherm said.

"What's wrong with it? Playing for the Homebrews a man ought to be entitled to a bottle of homebrew now and then, shouldn't he?" One of the front wheels of the car hit a hole in the dirt road and it almost made Garrett lose control. He grabbed the steering wheel and steadied the old Chevie.

153

Laura began to shrill from the back seat. "Daddy! Daddy!"

The two boys joined her. "Daddy! Daddy!"

Garrett only smiled. "It's okay, Ma, kids. Just a little old hole in the road. Sherm, there's a bottle opener in the glove compartment there. Let's have a snort. We deserve it after all we done today."

11

That August during threshing Garrett took the job of stacking straw for Sherm. His partner on the straw stack was Bachelor Bill Tamming. It was a miserably dusty job, but Sherm told them they could have an occasional bottle of homebrew so long as they did a good job.

Work on the stack was easy at first. All Garrett and Old Bill had to do was for one of them to push the straw around a little, and flatten it, while the other operated the blower. Dust wasn't too bad either.

As the day progressed and the stack rose, however, it got worse. All too soon the separator man had to take over the blower so both men could work the edges of the stack and do the tromping down. When the separator man was called away for a time then they really had to hump it, sometimes having to force themselves to work directly under the straw-clotted blast. Both men wore their shirts outside their overalls with the collars and the sleeves buttoned up tight to keep out the prickly chaff. Both wore dampened red handkerchiefs over the nose and mouth.

Garrett had nothing but contempt for his stacking partner. "Maybe I do drink a little," Garrett thought to himself, "but the things Bachelor Bill does are a scandal to the cowbirds."

Bachelor Bill still had his old bull brute hulk, could still put in a full day's work out in the fields, but over the years he had begun to act a bit queer. The more hair he lost the less sense he seemed to have.

As Garrett stompfed about on the springy yielding straw, scratching from here and pushing it there, he recalled some of the weird stories about Old Bill.

Everybody talked about how Old Bill had become such an awful tightwad. During the winter when he was out of work, he would visit from farm to farm much in the manner of a cowboy riding the grub-line, staying at each place at least a week, always beyond his welcome, until he got on everybody's nerves. The men didn't mind him so much because he usually pitched in with the chores, and sometimes he helped them get in the straw or ring the bull. But he ate like a hog—for fear it would be his last meal—and the women couldn't see that. At one place he once stayed two weeks. And he not only ate like a hog, with a bottomless pit for a stomach, he also chewed his way through the boss's month's supply of plug tobacco. At that point the lady of the house decided to fix him. She began to serve him smaller and smaller portions. To Old Bill's disgust the portion of meat on his plate at last almost disappeared. Then one morning he was gone. The boss said he thought he had heard Old Bill drive off in the night. The lady of the house was delighted. Several hours later, however, upon smelling something peculiar coming down the stairs, she began to wonder a little. She still hadn't made-up Old Bill's room, so she decided to take a peek. Well. She found the source of the smell all right. Old Bachelor Bill had neatly deposited a fine long turd exactly in the center of the white sheet. The lady of the house was horrified and blazing mad. And she was blocked. She couldn't very well tell anybody about it. Yes, Old Bill was also a pretty shrewd old beggar all right.

"And to think," Garrett thought, "that that's the nut who once wanted to marry my Laura. Let alone my June." Garrett shook his head. "You know, some-

157

times I think Old Bill was put into the world just to buck me. He always seems to be wanting what I want."

Already that day Old Bill had managed to cadge two good chews from Garrett's plug of tobacco, taking great big bites each time. "And I ain't had the heart to refuse him either."

Then a sly look came into Garrett's mild blue eyes, and he nodded to himself as he hunched around through the straw blasting out of the blower. "The next time he asks me for a chew it'll be different. You betcha. I'll fix him."

Around two o'clock the blower suddenly let up, the flying chaff ceased, and a silence fell. One of the belts on the separator had shredded and parted. The separator man said it would take some ten minutes to repair it.

"About time we had a break," Garrett said.

Old Bill nodded.

"Think I'll go down and take care of a little job."

Old Bill began to fidget around in the straw as if he were about to lay an egg. "Uhh, say, Garrett, I've run plumb out of plug tobacco somehow. Got an extry bite for me?"

"I've already give you two this morning. I thought you said you was gonna get a fresh plug from your car right after we ate dinner?"

Old Bill wiped his leathery old mouth with a

158

sidewise motion. "I couldn't find any. I was sure positive I had some too. Why, yup, I bought me several plugs at Rexroth's only last Satiddy."

"Too bad." Garrett began to descend the stack on an extension ladder.

Old Bill held the top of the ladder steady. "You have an extra chew, don't you, Garrett? You know a man can't stack straw without he has his whistle wet with a nice juicy chew."

"I'll see." Garrett in turn held the ladder steady at the bottom so Old Bill could come down.

"You know, man can't work in all that flying smut unless'n he chews."

"I know."

"Well then?"

"Ask Sherm for some. You're working for him, not me."

"You don't trust me."

"Can't say as I do."

"People say you're the easiest man in the world to get credit from. How come you won't give it to me?"

"You played wolf once too often with me, Bill." Garrett headed for a sheltered spot behind the hoghouse. "Remember?"

Old Bill followed him. "Oh, shecks, that. Why, Garrett, that was when we were nothing but antsy shitepokes. Full of the devil, is all. Can't hold that ag'in a man."

"I am." Garrett opened his trousers and after a pull or two let fly.

Old Bill let fly too. He stood working his jaws as if his teeth actually missed chewing tobacco. "You really ain't gonna borry me a chew then, huh, Garrett?"

"Welll . . ." Repressing an impulse to smile, Garrett quite casually got out his plug of tobacco from the bib pocket of his overalls and held it under the curving stream of his own water a second, then took a small bite. Garrett was quite careful to take his bite from a dry corner of the dark-brown cake of tobacco.

Old Bill gaggled. He was so astounded by what he had just seen his stream broke off.

"I always do this," Garrett said, "when I get the chance." Garrett held the plug out for Old Bill to take a bite. "Gives it a kind of a flavor. Especially when you're an old soak like me."

Old Bill buttoned himself up with angry fingers. "You mean to tell me them two chews this morning was treated the same way before you give 'em to me?"

"You betcha. It's the only way I can enjoy a chew." Again Garrett motioned for him to take a bite. "Don't you want some?"

Old Bill's leathery old face turned as red as the

wattles of a white Wyandotte cock. His big high red nose seemed to hump up even higher. He spotted a fork standing nearby and he dove for it. He leveled the fork's three shiny tines straight for Garrett's belly. "Garrett, for two cents I'd stick this into you, doing such a low mean dirty thing to me."

Garrett calmly put his plug away and kept right on making water. His stream didn't lessen a drop. He even smiled. "Better put that away, neighbor. Or somebody might get hurt."

Old Bill made a few practice jabs at Garrett, then hurled the fork aside. "Damn you, Garrett. I've got a half a notion to tell the judge about this. In fact, I might even take it to the United States Supreme Court." Old Bill stomped around on the cob-studded barnyard. "Yessiree, that's just what I'm gonna do."

"United States Supreme Court? I wouldn't do that if I was you."

"Why not? I got the right, ain't I?"

"Ha. With them that'd go over like a fart in church."

12

Four years later.

Things finally got so bad Garrett simply had to pull up stakes and try somewhere else.

He sold everything he had, including bills collectible, to pay off his debts; borrowed five hundred dollars from his cousin Sherm; then, packing Laura and the boys into his old grinding Chevie, set off for the land of eternal sunshine, California.

They landed in Bellflower where other bankrupt and heartbroken Siouxlanders sometimes settled.

The site of Bellflower had once been a series of endless lovely meadows covered with deep blue bellflowers. The bell-shaped flowers, for all their delicate form, also were tough, and they had given ground slowly to encroaching orange groves. But the city of Los Angeles kept growing and growing, so that more and more milk was needed, until gradually the dairies had taken over all the land between the orange groves, in some cases even supplanting them. That finally licked the bellflowers—though their name survived in the name of the town.

The best dairy operators turned out to be farmers from Siouxland, men who in many instances had been failures back home. The failures, however, had learned how to work in the rugged climes of the Upper Midlands, had learned the value of feeding their milk cows alfalfa grown on manure-enriched soils, had learned to milk the cows every twelve hours right on the dot. Some of the Siouxland-toughened farmers became rich in suddenly easy California.

One of the poorest Siouxlanders ever to arrive in Bellflower, and who was now the richest, was Hod Dickwinter.

Hod Dickwinter, for all his reputation as a pinchpenny, still had some sympathy left for the down and out, and it was he who gave Garrett a job as a stripper. Hod had also learned that a true down-and-outer never asked what the wages were, or tried to bargain with him for better pay, but simply took what was offered.

164

Garrett was a good stripper. As a plumber he'd developed powerful fingers and forearms. After the electric milking machine had drained the cow of most of her milk, Garrett came along and stripped her of her last few drops. Sometimes one of the back teats had a little extra to give, sometimes one of the front teats. Teats didn't always give in equal proportions. If a cow wasn't drained completely at each milking she slowly but surely tended to dry up.

The first year Garrett didn't drink much. He kept himself down to a bottle of beer a day, usually after the evening milking, before he went to bed. Milking time always started at four, both in the early morning and early afternoon. It meant Garrett had to go to bed early as well as take a nice catnap at noon. The regimen seemed to agree with him. He drank a lot of milk and ate well. Soon his pink color returned and his eyes became a steady blue. About six months after he started working steady Garrett began to jolly Laura again, to her delight. He especially liked to jolly her after his lazy catnap at noon when the boys were gone to school and he and the good wife were deliciously home alone.

Laura came to love her new country. She couldn't get over how many flowers there were everywhere. What astonished her even more was that she could grow roses in the wintertime if she took care.

"It's Eden at last," Laura commented one day as

she looked out of her kitchen window onto her own garden of colors.

"What is?"

"California. The flowers."

"Don't smell much though."

"What don't?"

"The flowers. You gotta have a nose as big as a pair of mule ears to get even so much as a little bitty pinch of a smell."

"Well, maybe so. But the flowers sure look good."

"T'while the cowplop stinks twice as bad." Garrett lit his pipe and fitted it between his teeth. Over the years he had smoked his pipe so much in the same corner of his mouth, holding it between his teeth as he worked, that the pipestem had worn a neat groove or gap into his teeth. He could close his jaws tight and still have room for the pipestem in the worn gap. "Yeh. Fella was saying down at the milk barn the other day that the mountains around are all rotting. Coming apart like an over-dried clod of dirt. Well, it don't surprise me none. Weather around here is like lukewarm tea. Nature here don't get enough exercise to stay in shape. A real hot spell now and then and then a durn good freeze would do it a world of good. Stretch it and toughen it."

"You don't like it here then. In California."

"It's all right."

166

"The boys're happy."

"It's all right."

"We're eating and paying all our bills as we go."

"Now that I got a steady paycheck without having to ask for it, eh?"

Laura pulled her corset down over her chunk of a stomach, cast Garrett a searching look, and fell silent.

Garrett puffed musingly on his pipe. "By God, they even have to import the hay here. Why? Because the local hay ain't got the gaff."

A tear showed in Laura's eye and after a moment she went outside to tend her flowers.

13

One Sunday, after church, Garrett and Laura and the two boys took a little trip into Los Angeles and beyond. Garrett didn't like the coppery mist hanging over the city and lit up his curve-stem pipe against it. The air was a little better when they got to Hollywood. Laura exclaimed again about all the lovely strange flowers, while the boys were agog over the many white glittering open-sky buildings. When they climbed Hollywood Boulevard and parked for a look out over the citied plain below, Garrett let his pipe go out and just sat and sat.

On the way home they noticed the traffic more

169

closely, the kind of cars and the kind of people who drove them. Every possible make of car in the world, every kind of shape and color, whizzed past them. People always took the twisting turns with squealing tires. The cars stopped hard on the red signal, tail up; they started hard on the green signal, tail down.

The drivers of the cars caught Garrett's eye. A third of the little speedy cars were driven by blonds, sitting alone with their hair done up like bobtail race horses, all of them lovely to look at.

Garrett finally remarked, "Well, here's one place where King Solomon would go nuts."

"Because of all the beautiful temples, Dad?" Harvey asked from the back seat.

"No, not quite that."

"Because of all the rich people?" Chester asked.

"No."

"What then?" Laura said.

"No." Garrett gave Laura a sly wink. "No, mostly because of all the pretty women. Here in Hollywood he would have to marry a million of them to feel satisfied. Not just a little old measly thousand."

"Garrett. You."

Garrett patted Laura on her chunk of a belly. "The old gray mare, she ain't what she used to be, nosiree, but, my how she can still eat the oats, huh?"

"Garrett."

14

At work, Garrett got along most of the time with his boss, Hod Dickwinter. Hod often reminded Garrett of Old Bill Tamming. Hod was also a tall and balding fellow, though where Old Bill shambled as he walked Hod hurried. Hod had a sly flat-lipped smile that was very deceptive, because when he got mad he was a rager. He could get so mottled mad sometimes his face resembled a handful of diseased liver. Most of his rages had to do with waste. Spill as much as one drop of milk and he was onto you like a police dog with rabies. He carried only a small amount of insurance on the place on the theory that if he kept close watch a fire would never really get started. And if a fire did break out, he was sure to be close around somewhere to put it out before it got much of a start. Hence he was death on smoking. All pipes and all smokes whatsoever had to be out when one entered his gates. He'd even had a huge sign painted over the entrance to his dairy which read: "You can smoke all you want to in Hell, but not here."

A couple of times Garrett had himself a quiet smoke in the misty milk room where the floor was always wet. Once, an hour after Garrett had had such a smoke, Hod had come in and immediately began to rant and rave. "Who's been smoking around here? Huh? Damn him. I'll send him straight to hell with a swift kick in his rotten prat, I will. Who done that? Huh? huh?"

Garrett smiled quietly from where he sat on his three-legged stripping stool. "I done it."

Hod jumped over him, fists upraised. "I could . . . I could . . . Man, I could fire you for that, you know that?" Hod's face beetled up all red.

"I know."

"Listen, Garrett, it's only because you're the best stripper I ever had that I don't fire you."

"Glad to hear that."

"Dammit, Garrett, don't smoke around here again on the premises, d' hear?" Hod stomped around in his big red wobbly rubber boots. "I'd much rather you'd sneak a nip on the bottle, if you must sneak something."

"I wasn't sneaking. I figure it's pretty safe to smoke where it's so wet and all."

"No, no, no! You can't smoke here. If the insurance company ever hears of it the rates will go up."

Garrett smiled quietly. His pet pipe began to lay heavy in the bib of his overalls.

One Frisian-Holstein cow named Old Bouncy took the longest to strip. The near front teat and the far teat always had a pint or so left over after the milking machine got through with her. Over a period of several months, Garrett began to notice something. The two teats seemed to gain a little in capacity. There always seemed to be a little more left over. The better he stripped the two teats the more they had to give. In fact it was getting to be a chore to clean her. Garrett considered the idea of leaving some left over in them so they would begin to dry a little, and so fall back even with the other two. Of course he could also try to get the other two to draw up even with the full ones. If he did that then he'd really make a producer out of Old Bouncy. Good Old Bouncy with her big swinging bouncing bag.

He was sitting early one morning stripping Old Bouncy, head into her black flank, pail between his knees, one foot spraddled out over the gutter, when his thoughts for some reason switched all the way

173

back to the old days in Siouxland. He saw June Memling lying on the grass beside him again, her lovely breasts standing up like little silver bells in the moonlight, he kissing them, even suckling them a little. Once again he smelled the heady fumes of June. Perhaps it was the way he stripped Bouncy's teats between his thumb and forefinger that did it, but anyway there June was. She was so clear in his mind's eye it was like she was right there in the cow barn with him. In plain sight for him to see.

"June, June," he said aloud, "why did we do it?"

Then he caught himself, blinked his eyes in the hair on the cow's flank, and turned his full attention to the problem of the uneven teats.

He hungered for a good snort of spiked beer.

But of course that was out of the question as long as he was doing so well with Hod Dickwinter. One drink on the job and he was finished. He had the whole drinking problem licked as long as he had his bottle of beer for a nightcap.

He also hungered for his pipe.

After a minute, looking up and down the cow stalls to make sure no one was around, he muttered, "One little puff on my pipe won't hurt none. There's still a little crumble of tobacco left in the bowl. I'll just smoke that through. Hod almost never comes back here after he's finished with the milking machines."

He lit his curved-stem pipe and, holding his head away from Old Bouncy, went back to stripping. The pipestem fit comfortably in the worn gap in his teeth. The soft fumes from it tasted sweet, almost as sweet as corn silk smelled in the fall.

Garrett pulled away steadily.

He paused once to adjust the belt buckle to his stripping stool. Hod Dickwinter had invented a way of strapping a milk stool to a stripper's backside. When a stripper settled beside a cow his milk stool fell neatly into place under him as he sat down. When a stripper got up, his milk stool stuck out behind him like a miniature three-pronged battering ram.

Presently Old Bouncy turned her white-black head around in the stanchion and wondered what the strange smell was. After a moment, as if to show him what she thought about it, she humped her back and watered in the gutter.

Garrett almost had the two overfull teats done, when there was a heavy wobbling step behind him down the alley. Holy Habakkuk! Hod Dickwinter. Without losing a stroke, clamping down on the jump in his knees, Garrett, too casually, turned his head to hide his pipe against the cow's flank.

Before Hod could roar that he was smelling smoke somewhere, Old Bouncy made her move. The bowl of Garrett's pipe lay hot on her flank, and up she went, the whole rear end of her. Before she came down, she also lashed out with a powerful paired kick. The paired kick caught Garrett on the side of the head. It stunned him, and he fell on his back into the shining wet gutter. Again Old Bouncy went up, this time missing him. But on coming down both her hooves landed on his belly. Somehow one of her hooves slipped behind the belt to his stripping stool and a hock got caught in the belt buckle. Old Bouncy, scared at having her hoof entangled, began to kick frantically, up, down, in, out. Everything went wild then.

There was a soft taut sound as if a leather pouch had been punctured. One of Old Bouncy's split hooves came down just hard enough to break into Garrett's skinny belly. When Old Bouncy tried to pull her hoof out of Garrett, the hock again caught, this time on one of the coils of his intestines. She jerked, jerked, jerked. When her hoof finally did come out, his intestines were tightly wrapped around it. Old Bouncy became even more frightened at this. She began to bellow, really began to bounce around. And the more she jumped the more she ripped out Garrett's guts. Garrett's intestines piled up all over the place.

Garrett never let out a peep. He looked on at what was happening to him with slowly growing

176

astonishment. Only at last did he grab hold of her wildly kicking leg and try to keep her from tearing him completely inside out.

Hod began to yell. He yelled like the steady relentless blowing of a piercing steam whistle. Then Hod's mouth snapped to and he came to his senses. He grabbed up a loose fence post standing just inside the barn door, and running around through the feeding alley, clubbed Old Bouncy one awful clout between her black horns, and down she dropped, stunned, unconscious. More help came running and only then did they get Garrett untangled from Old Bouncy's hoof.

At the hospital, the doctors washed off Garrett's intestines, gave him penicillin, sewed him up, treated him for shock, and put him to bed. No vital organs inside had been ruptured or seriously damaged. Just the skin and the belly muscles. The doctors said he was very lucky.

For a week Garrett did very well; even seemed to be gaining.

Then, one evening, very tired of it all, Garrett closed his eyes and died.

A picture of the still-living Prince of Wales happened to be in the newspaper the day of Garrett's funeral. The peoples of the world were once again being reminded that the Prince of Wales had given up a kingdom for the sake of love. Everybody who viewed Garrett's body commented on the strange fact that the face they saw in the coffin was exactly like the face they saw in the newspaper.

April-October, 1963
Blue Mound
Luverne, Minnesota

ABOUT THE AUTHOR

Frederick Feikema Manfred was born January 6, 1912, on a Siouxland farm north of Doon, Iowa, in Rock township, just a few miles from the Minnesota and South Dakota borders. Mr. Manfred is the oldest of six brothers. His mother died in 1929; his father now lives in California.

He was educated in northwest Iowa until he attended Calvin College, Grand Rapids, Michigan, from which he graduated in 1934. From then until 1937 he wandered back and forth across America, from New York to Los Angeles, stopping off now and then to fill jobs which ran the entire gamut of temporary employment. In May, 1937, he became a reporter for the *Minneapolis Journal*. In 1939 he did social work and opinion polls. In 1942 he married Maryanna Shorba; they now have three children, Freya, Marya, and Frederick.

In 1943 Mr. Manfred, concluding that it was now or never, devoted full time and energy to writing. Since then he has published fifteen books, including the novels LORD GRIZZLY, RIDERS OF JUDGMENT, CONQUERING HORSE, SCARLET PLUME, MORNING RED, and the trilogy WANDERLUST. He has received many grants and writing fellowships, from such sponsors as the American Academy of Arts and Letters and the Huntington Hartford Foundation. Until 1951 he wrote under the pen name of Feike Feikema, an old Frisian family name, of which Frederick Manfred is a translation. In Frisian genealogy his full name is Feike Feikes Feikema VII.

Mr. Manfred has lived in the Upper Midlands, mostly in Siouxland, all his life. He likes gardening, fixing fence, and chopping wood; and enjoys taking long rambling walks alone through the countryside.